"Women Aren't About To Line Up To Have My Baby."

"You are so without a clue. Look at you!" And she did. She leaned back and looked at him with a thoroughness that reminded him how much she'd changed. "Women find that whole rugged loner thing a complete turn-on."

"What a load of bull!"

She made an impatient tsking sound with her tongue. "You get to the city occasionally…or at least you used to. You have to feel women looking you over. You can't *not* know you're like their living, breathing, outback fantasy."

Fantasy? Big deal. What he needed was reality, female and available.

"Name one who'd have my baby," he said roughly.

She blinked slowly and edged back another inch. Which was when he noticed that he'd gotten right in her face. Close enough that he heard her indrawn breath. The only sound in the intense silence, until she spoke.

"I would."

Dear Reader,

July is a month known for its heat and fireworks, as well as the perfect time to take that vacation. Well, why not take a break and enjoy some hot sparks with a Silhouette Desire? We've got six extraordinary romances to share with you this month, starting with *Betrayed Birthright* by Sheri WhiteFeather. This seventh title in our outstanding DYNASTIES: THE ASHTONS series is sure to reveal some unbelievable facts about this scandalous family.

USA TODAY bestselling author Maureen Child wraps up her fabulous THREE-WAY WAGER series with *The Last Reilly Standing*. Or is he getting down on bended knee? And while some series are coming to a close, new ones are just beginning, such as our latest installment of the TEXAS CATTLEMAN'S CLUB: THE SECRET DIARY. Cindy Gerard kicks off this six-book continuity with *Black-Tie Seduction*. Also starting this month is Bronwyn Jameson's PRINCES OF THE OUTBACK. These Australian hunks really need to be tamed, beginning with *The Rugged Loner.*

A desert beauty in love with a tempting beast. That's the theme of Nalini Singh's newest release, *Craving Beauty*—a story not to be missed. And the need to break a long-standing family curse leads to an attraction that's just *Like Lightning*, an outstanding romance by Charlene Sands.

Here's hoping you enjoy all the fireworks Silhouette Desire has to offer you…this month and all year long!

Best,

Melissa Jeglinski

Melissa Jeglinski
Senior Editor
Silhouette Desire

Please address questions and book requests to:
Silhouette Reader Service
U.S.: 3010 Walden Ave., P.O. Box 1325, Buffalo, NY 14269
Canadian: P.O. Box 609, Fort Erie, Ont. L2A 5X3

THE RUGGED LONER

BRONWYN JAMESON

Published by Silhouette Books
America's Publisher of Contemporary Romance

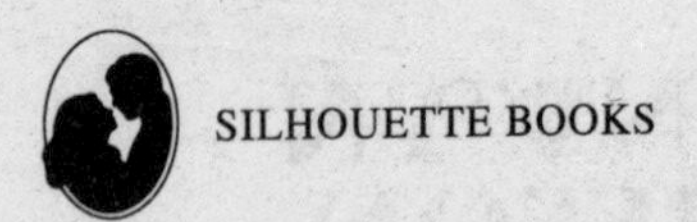

ISBN 0-373-76666-1

THE RUGGED LONER

This edition published by arrangement with Harlequin Books S.A.

Visit Silhouette Books at www.eHarlequin.com

Printed in U.S.A.

Books by Bronwyn Jameson

Silhouette Desire

In Bed with the Boss's Daughter #1380
Addicted to Nick #1410
Zane: The Wild One #1452
Quade: The Irresistible One #1487
A Tempting Engagement #1571
Beyond Control #1596
Just a Taste #1645
**The Rugged Loner* #1666

*Princes of the Outback

BRONWYN JAMESON

spent much of her childhood with her head buried in a book. As a teenager, she discovered romance novels, and it was only a matter of time before she turned her love of reading them into a love of writing them. Bronwyn shares an idyllic piece of the Australian farming heartland with her husband and three sons, a thousand sheep, a dozen horses, assorted wildlife and one kelpie dog. She still chooses to spend her limited downtime with a good book. Bronwyn loves to hear from readers. Write to her at bronwyn@bronwynjameson.com.

OUTBACK GLOSSARY

Akubra—famous brand of Australian outback/ cattlemen's hat

Barakoolie Ridge—a landmark on Kameruka Downs

Boolah—location of a set of cattle yards on Kameruka Downs

cleanskin—an unbranded beast (cattle)

hoon—wild, fast driver

Kameruka Downs—the Carlisle family's outback station

Killarney—another Carlisle-owned station

King Air—one of the Carlisle company planes

Koomah Crossing—the nearest settlement to Kameruka Downs

muster—roundup

ringer—an experienced musterer (cowboy, stockman)

Ruby Creek—a nearby station, famed for its race meeting

station—large grazing property

stock camp—group of stockmen out on a muster (on big stations they can be away from home, camping out for weeks)

swag—bedroll, used when camping

Territory—the Northern Territory, an Australian "state"

ute—utility; pickup truck

weaners—young cattle, recently weaned from their mothers

Prologue

Charles Carlisle knew he was dying. His family denied it. The herd of medical specialists they'd employed kept skirting around the flanks of the truth like a team of well-trained cattle dogs, but Chas knew his number had come up.

If the tumor mushrooming inside his brain didn't finish him off, the intense radiation therapy he was about to commence would. The only other soul willing to accept the truth was his good mate Jack Konrads. Not surprising since as an estate lawyer Jack dealt with human mortality every day of his working life.

Chas supposed his lawyer friend got to deal with plenty of unusual will clauses, too, because his face remained impressively deadpan as he digested the changes just requested by Chas. Carefully he set the single sheet of paper aside. "I assume you've discussed this with your sons?"

"So they can make my last months a living hell?" Chas snorted. "They'll find out once I'm six feet under!"

"You don't think they deserve some forewarning? Twelve months is precious little time to produce a baby from scratch—even if any one of them was already married and planning to start a family."

"You suggest I should give them time to wiggle out of this?" They were clever enough, his sons. Too clever at times for their own good. "Alex and Rafe are past thirty. They need a decent shove or they'll never settle down."

Brow furrowed with a deep frown, Jack perused his written instructions again. "This wording doesn't seem to exclude Tomas…."

"No exclusions. It's the same for all of them."

"You don't have to prove anything to those boys," Jack said slowly, still frowning. "They know you don't play favorites. You've always treated them as if they're all your sons by birth. They've grown into fine men, Chas."

Yes, they were sons to make any father proud, but in recent years they'd grown apart, each wrapped up in his own world, too busy, too self-involved. This clause would fix that. It would rekindle the spirit of kinship he'd watched grow with the boys as they raced their ponies over the flat grasslands of their outback station. Later they'd roped cleanskin bulls and corporate competitors with the same ruthless determination. He was counting on that get-it-done attribute when it came time to execute this will clause.

"It has to be the same for all three," he repeated resolutely. He couldn't exclude Tomas—didn't want to exclude Tomas.

"It's been barely two years since Brooke was killed."

"And the longer he stays buried in grief, the harder the task of digging his way out." Jaw set, Chas leaned forward and met his friend's eyes. "That, I know."

If *his* father hadn't forced his hand—tough love, he'd called it—Chas would have buried himself in the outback after his first wife's death. He wouldn't have been forced overseas to manage his father's British interests and he wouldn't have met a wild Irish-born beauty named Maura Keane and her two young sons.

He wouldn't have fallen completely and utterly in love.

He wouldn't have married her and completed his family with their own son, Tomas. Their son whose grief over *his* young wife's death was turning him as hard and remote as his outback home. Tomas needed some mighty tough love before it was too late.

"Does Maura know about this?" Jack asked carefully.

"No, and that's the way I want it to stay. You know she won't approve."

For a long moment Jack regarded him over the top of his glasses. "Hell of a way to take all their minds off grieving for you."

Chas scowled. "That's not what this is about. It'll get them working together to find the best solution. My family needs a shake-up, Tomas most of all."

"And what if your plan backfires? What if the boys reject this clause and walk away from their inheritance? Do you want the Carlisle assets split up and sold off?"

"That won't happen."

"They won't like this—"

"They don't have to like it. I suspect I'll hear their objections from beyond the pearly gates, but they'll do it. Not for the inheritance—" Chas fixed his friend with his trademark gaze, steel-hard and unwavering. "They'll do it for their mother."

And that was the biggest, strongest motivation for this added clause to the last will and testament of Charles Tomas

McLachlan Carlisle. He wanted more than his sons working together. He didn't only want to see them take a chance at settled, family happiness. This was for Maura. A grandchild, born within twelve months of his death, to bring a smile to her sad eyes, to break her growing isolation.

He wanted, in death, to achieve what he'd never been able to do in life: to make his adored wife happy.

"This is my legacy to Maura, Jack."

And the only thing out of a multibillion-dollar empire that would be worth an Irish damn to her.

One

Six months later

Angelina Mori didn't mean to eavesdrop. If, at the last minute, she hadn't remembered the solemnity of the occasion she would have charged into the room in her usual forthright fashion and she wouldn't have heard a thing.

But she did remember the occasion—this morning's burial, this afternoon's reading of the will, the ensuing meeting between Charles Carlisle's heirs—and she paused and steadied herself to make a decorous entrance into the Kameruka Downs library.

Which is how she came to overhear the three deep, male voices. Three voices as familiar to Angie's ear as those of her own two brothers.

"You heard what Konrads said. We don't all have to do

this." Alex, the eldest, sounded as calm and composed as ever. "It's my responsibility."

"News flash." Rafe's mocking drawl hadn't changed a bit in the time she'd been gone. "Your advanced age doesn't make you the expert or the one in charge of this. How about we toss a coin. Heads, you—"

"The hell you say. We're in this together. One in, all in." Tomas's face, she knew, would be as hard and expressionless as his voice. Heartbreakingly different to the man she remembered from… Was it only five years ago? It seemed so much longer, almost another lifetime.

"A nice sentiment, little bro', but aren't you forgetting something?" Rafe asked. "It takes two to make a baby."

Angie didn't drop the tray of sandwiches she held, but it was a near thing. Heart hammering, she pulled the tray tight against her waist and steadied it with a white-knuckled grip. The rattling plates quieted; the pounding of her heart didn't.

And despite what she'd overheard—or maybe because of it—she didn't slink away.

With both hands occupied, she couldn't knock on the half-closed door. Instead she nudged it open with one knee and cleared her throat. Loudly. Twice. Because now the voices were raised in strident debate on who was going to do this—*get married? have a baby? in order to inherit?*—and how.

Holy Henry Moses.

Angie cleared her throat a third time, and three pairs of intensely irritated, blue eyes turned her way. The Carlisle brothers. "Princes of the Outback" according to this week's headlines, but only because some hack had once dubbed their father's extensive holdings in the Australian outback "Carlisle's Kingdom."

Angie had grown up by their rough-and-tumble side. They might look like the tabloid press's idea of Australian royalty, but they didn't fool her for a second.

Princes? Ha!

"What?" at least two *princes* barked now.

"Sorry to intrude, but you've been holed up in here for yonks. I thought you might need some sustenance." She deposited her tray in the center of the big oak desk and her hip on its edge. Then she reached for the bottle of forty-year-old Glenfiddich—pilfered from their father's secret stash—and swirled the rich, amber contents in the light. More than half-full. Amazing. "I thought you'd have made a bigger dent in this."

Alex squinted at the glass in his hand as if he'd forgotten its existence. Rafe winked and held his out for a refill. Broad back to the room, hands shoved deep into the pockets of his black dress trousers, Tomas acknowledged neither the whisky nor her arrival.

And no one so much as glanced at the sandwiches. They didn't want sustenance. They wanted her to leave so they could continue their discussion.

Tough.

She slid her backside further onto the desk, took her time selecting a corn beef and pickle triangle, then arched a brow at the room in general. "So, what's this about a baby?"

Tomas's shoulders tensed. Alex and Rafe exchanged a look.

"It's no use pretending nothing's going on," she said around her first bite. "I overheard you talking."

For a long moment she thought they'd pull the old boys' club number, buttoning up in front of the girl. Except this girl had spent her whole childhood tearing around Kameruka Downs in the dust of these three males and her two brothers. Sadly outnumbered, she'd learned to chase hard and to never give up. She glanced sideways at Tomas's back. At least not until she was completely beaten.

"Well?" she prompted.

Rafe, bless his heart, relented. "What do you think, Ange? Would you—"

"This is supposed to be private," Alex said pointedly.

"You don't think Ange's opinion is valuable? She's a woman."

"Thank you for noticing," Angie murmured. From the corner of her eye she watched Tomas who had never noticed, while she fought two equally strong, conflicting urges. One part of her ached to slide off the desk and wrap him and his tightly held pain in a big old-fashioned hug. The other wanted to slug him one for ignoring her.

"Would you have somebody's baby...for money?"

What? Her attention swung from the still and silent figure by the window and back to Rafe. She swallowed. "Somebody's?"

"Yeah." Rafe cocked a brow. "Take our little brother, the hermit, for example. He says he'd pay and since that's—"

"Enough," Alex cut in.

Unnecessarily, as it happened, because a second later—so quick, Angie didn't see it coming—Tomas held Rafe by the shirtfront. The two harsh flat syllables he uttered would never have emanated from any prince's mouth.

Alex separated them, but Tomas only stayed long enough for a final curt directive to his brothers. "You do this your way, I'll do it mine. I don't need your approval."

He didn't slam the door on his way out, and it occurred to Angie that that would have shown too much passion, too much heat, for the cold, remote stranger the youngest Carlisle had become.

"I guess my opinion is beside the point now," she said carefully.

Rafe coughed out a laugh. "Only if you think Mr. Congeniality can find himself a woman."

Angie's heart thumped against her ribs. Oh, he could. She had no doubts about that. Tomas Carlisle might have forgotten how to smile, but he could take his big, hard body and I've-been-hurt-bad attitude into any bar and choose from the top shelf. Without any mention of the Carlisle billions.

A chill shivered through her skin as she put down the remains of her sandwich. "He won't do anything stupid, will he?"

"Not if we stop him."

Alex shook his head. "Leave him be, Rafe."

"Do you really think he's in any mood to make a discriminating choice?" Rafe made an impatient sound, not quite a laugh, not quite a snort. "What the hell was Dad thinking anyway? He should have left Tomas right out of this!"

"Maybe he wanted to give him a shake-up," Alex said slowly.

"The kind that sends him out looking to cut a deal with the first bar-bunny he happens upon?"

Angie stood so swiftly, her head spun. Whoa. Breathing deeply, she leaned against the desk. It was okay. Kameruka Downs was two hours of black dust and corrugated roads from the nearest bar. Even if Tomas did decide to hightail it into Koomah Crossing, he wouldn't make closing time.

She exhaled slowly and settled back on the desk. "Confession time, guys. I really only overheard one slice of your earlier discussion, so who'd like to fill me in on the whole story?"

* * *

Once, on a bet, Angie had raced Tomas and her brother Carlo from the homestead to the waterhole, blindfolded. Remembering that experience fifteen years ago made tonight's steep descent a veritable walk in the park. A three-quarter moon rode high in the sky, casting enough light for Angie to pick a surefooted path through the scrub. Behind a bandanna blindfold there'd been nothing but intense black, yet she'd closed her eyes and run.

Anything to prove herself less of a girl.

You're part feral goat, the boys had spat in disgust as they handed over her winnings, and it had taken Angie years to realize that comparison wasn't exactly flattering.

Her smile, wry and reminiscent, faded as she neared her destination. *Moment of truth, sister.* She rubbed warming hands up and down her goose-bumped arms. She would bet the vintage silk-georgette dress she'd vainly not changed out of—despite the chill night and a setting more suited to jeans—that Tomas had retreated to his usual lair.

And when you find him, you say your piece and you make sure he listens. You don't let him turn his back.

She'd seen Tomas several times since her return from Italy a week earlier. At the hospital before his father passed away, at the memorial service held largely for his city business associates, at Alex's Sydney home afterward. Yet he'd managed to evade anything beyond a quick consoling hug and a few token words of sympathy.

So she'd stayed on at Kameruka Downs after the private funeral, begging a lift back to Sydney on the corporate jet with Alex and Rafe, instead of returning on the afternoon charter arranged for other mourners. She had to talk to Tomas, one on one. She had to set things straight between them.

This had nothing to do with the disturbing clause in Charles's will that she'd just learned about in the library. This was about guilt and regret and failing to be the kind of friend she wanted to be. It was about closure, too, and moving on with her life.

And it promised to be damn-near the toughest thing she'd ever done. Tougher even than the night she'd confronted Tomas with her opinion on his upcoming marriage…and that had been Tough with a capital T!

It wasn't that she hadn't liked Brooke. They'd been close friends at school. Tomas had met his future wife at Angie's eighteenth birthday party, on a night when *she'd* dressed and preened and set herself on being noticed as a woman instead of his wild-child pseudosister.

Instead—the supreme irony—he'd fallen into complete blinker-eyed besottedness with her petite and delicate friend. And eighteen months later he hadn't wanted to hear Angie's opinion on Brooke's suitability to life in the outback. He loved Brooke. He married Brooke.

And *that* had been one tough challenge Angie couldn't face.

Instead of accepting the bridesmaid's gig, she'd taken off on a backpacking jaunt to Europe. Her grand adventure had started as an impulsive escape from pain and envy, from her fear that she wouldn't make it through "does anyone have just cause" without jumping to her feet and yelling, "You bet I do! He's supposed to be mine!"

She'd missed the wedding and, worse, she'd missed Brooke's funeral. But now she was back, needing to make peace with her conscience. She doubted she could make peace with the flint-hard stranger Tomas had become, but she had to try.

"Moment of truth," she muttered, out loud this time,

as she ducked under a branch into the clearing beside the waterhole.

Slowly she scanned the darkness and the empty shadows, before hauling herself up onto a rock overhang. On sure feet she climbed higher to the secret cave. Peered inside.

Backed-up breath huffed from her lungs.

Nothing. *Damn.*

Disappointment expanded, tightening her chest as she slowly descended to the ground. She'd made a deal with herself, a deal about finding him and getting this over with tonight. How could she do that when he wasn't here?

Swearing softly, she turned to leave.

Or perhaps he simply didn't want to be found....

Her eyes narrowed. Perhaps Tomas hadn't changed completely. Perhaps now, as in the past, he wasn't completely alone down here.

Angie allowed herself a small smile before she lifted both pinkies to her pursed lips and whistled.

Tomas figured someone—most likely Angie—would come looking for him. He'd counted on the night hiding his secluded location. He hadn't counted on her whistling his dog.

Ajay responded with a high-pitched whine of suspicion. Rough translation: *You can whistle—point in your favor—but I'm no pushover. I'm a red heeler; I protect my boss. You better proceed with caution.*

Angie didn't.

The quick tread of her approach was as incisive and uninhibited as her personality. Loose gravel dislodged by her climbing feet splished into the water below, and Tomas saw the hair rise along Ajay's spine. Under his restraining hand he felt a warning growl vibrate through the dog's tense body. It was a measure of his own snarled mood that he actually considered letting the heeler loose.

He didn't.

His muttered "Stay" was probably for the dog—God knows Angie wouldn't take a lick of notice!

As if to prove his point, she appeared out of the darkness and used his shoulder to steady herself as she dropped down at his side. The floaty skirt of her dress settled around her legs where they dangled over the rock ledge, a flutter of feminine contrast to the rugged setting and the worn denim stretched over his thighs alongside.

"Did you consider I might want to be alone?" he asked, surprising himself with the even tone of his voice. Ever since Jack Konrads read out that newly added will clause, tension had snarled through his blood and his flesh. An anger that had whipped the hollow numbness of grief and loss into something hot and taut and hazardous.

"Yes," she said simply, with a quick flash of smile.

Although that could have been for Ajay, because on the heels of the smile came a softly crooned note of surprise. Her hand slid from his shoulder down his arm—from rolled-up shirtsleeve to skin—as she leaned around him to take a better look. "While I was clambering up here, I kinda thought you mightn't have Sergeant anymore."

"He died."

For the tiniest hint of time, she stilled. Then the pressure of her hand on his forearm changed, a tactile expression of her next words. "I'm sorry to hear that."

"He got old."

"As we all do." She leaned forward. "Well, aren't you handsome." And started to reach—

"Best you don't do that."

"I'm only saying hello."

And wouldn't you know it? His wary-natured heeler didn't take a piece out of her hand. Tomas breathed a tad easier…but only a tad. He was still struggling to reconcile the Angie he knew—the annoying, exasperating, teenage tomboy—with this exotic, alien creature who'd returned from Europe.

She wore dresses, for pity's sake. She'd straightened her unruly curls into one of those city-girl do's, all sleek and dark and glossy. And every time she moved he heard the delicate tinkle of the jewelry she wore on her wrists and ankle.

Hell, she even had some kind of rings on her toes. And as for the perfume…

"What's with the perfume?"

"Excuse me?"

Yeah, excuse him. He hadn't meant to say it, the question that blared in his brain every time he breathed around her. Ever since that first day he saw her again—*hell, was that only last week?*—when she'd rushed down the hallway of the hospital to throw her arms around him, to hug him and hold him and leak tears and words and more tears into his shirt.

Except instead of feeling comforted, he'd dragged in air rich with this perfume and he'd felt her curves against his body and he'd tensed. His hands had set her aside, this woman who no longer felt anything like Angie should.

She'd changed when all he wanted was someone—something—to stay the same. To anchor him to the past that fate kept wrenching away.

"You smell…different," he accused now. She smelled different, she looked different, and right now in the dark he swore she was looking at him different, too. "You've changed, Dash."

His use of her childhood nickname surprised a laugh from her full lips. With a clink of bracelets, her hand slid away from his arm, thank God, and into her lap. "Wow. There's a blast from the past. No one's called me Dash in…forever."

Yeah, forever about summed it up.

Forever since the last time she'd followed him down here, bent on telling him how the outback and Brooke would never see eye to eye. Like he hadn't known. And like he'd not been young enough and cocky enough to think it wouldn't make a difference.

"It's only been five years, but you're right. I've changed, you've changed, everything's changed," she said softly, and suddenly the darkness seemed more intense. Suffocatingly so. "I'm sorry about your father, that he got so sick and had to suffer and that the last weeks were so hard on you all. I'm sorry I wasn't here, and I hope—"

"You didn't have to come down here to tell me that. I've heard it more than enough times this last week."

"Yeah, well, you haven't heard it from me. At least not without cutting me off midsentence and walking away." She angled her chin in that determined way she had. "I have more to say, actually, and this time I want you to stay put until I finish."

Something about her tone and the sympathetic darkness of her eyes alerted him to what might be on her mind, and he started to move, to get the hell out of the conversation. But she put her hand on his knee, stopping him. It was the Angie-of-old, exasperating and annoying and not letting him get away without first saying her piece.

"Did you get my letter?" she asked.

Yeah, he'd gotten the letter she'd written after Brooke

was killed. What did she expect him to say? Thank you for your kind thoughts? They really helped me cope when my heart had been ripped bleeding from my chest.

"I hated that a lousy letter was all I could send," she continued. "I wish I could have been here. I wish I could have found better words."

"It wouldn't have made any difference."

"It would have to me." She moved her hand—had she always been such a toucher, or had that changed, too?—this time covering his fist where it sat clenched on this thigh. She squeezed his tense knuckles. "I wasn't here for you when it mattered, when I should have been. What kind of friend does that make me?"

Was he supposed to answer that? Or just sit here like some priest in an outdoors confessional and let her talk so she'd feel better about herself?

He hoped she wasn't after absolution, because that sure wasn't anything he was qualified to give!

"Your friendship matters to me. Are we still friends, T.J.?"

His childhood nickname, but it sounded all wrong on her lips because she'd leaned closer, her arm pressed warm and soft against his, her perfume a sensuous drift of woman in his nostrils. And then she did that squeezing thing again, probably meaning to reassure him but only screwing his tension up another notch.

He wrested his hand away, put hers back in her lap. "If it makes you feel better, why the hell not?"

"Yeesh, Tomas!" She let her breath go sharply, exasperated. "Can't you at least pretend to accept sympathy from a friend? Would that hurt so very much?"

When he didn't answer, she shook her head slowly. The slippery ends of her hair skimmed against his bare forearm as if coolly mocking one of the reasons he didn't feel like she was his friend. This strange awareness that he didn't want or like or need.

The disturbing notion that little Angie had grown up into a woman...and his man's body wouldn't stop noticing.

"That's all I came down here to say," she said abruptly. "Accept it or don't. I'll leave you to enjoy your pity party alone."

She'd already started to rise, not using his shoulder for leverage this time, and Tomas should have let her go. Shouldn't have felt the irrational need to ask, "That's it? That's all you came down here to say?"

"Oh, boy." Beside him she stilled, then her laughter rumbled, as soft and husky-dark as the night. "I really want to say, yes, that's it. I really, *really* know I should."

"But?"

"But you wouldn't have baited me to stay unless you needed to talk." She sank back down and he felt her gaze on his face, felt it turn serious. "It's that will clause, isn't it?"

"You don't think that's worth throwing a pity party over?"

She didn't answer that question, not directly. Instead she sighed and shook her head. "It's worth worrying about, sure. But wouldn't you be better off back at the homestead talking it through with your brothers?"

Tomas snorted. "What's there to talk through?"

"For a start, there's some worry about how you'll choose a mother for this baby you think you have to produce."

"There's no 'think' about it."

"My understanding is that only one of you needs do this. One baby between the three of you."

"You think I'd leave it up to my brothers? When I stand to lose all this?" He gestured around him, indicating the land that was more than a family legacy. Kameruka Downs was the only place he'd ever wanted to live and all he had left since the plane crash that took his wife's life, his happiness, his future.

"Your brothers know this place is everything to you," Angie said softly.

Wrong. It wasn't everything; it was the only thing.

"Alex says he's going to marry Susannah."

"Yeah, right. When they both can schedule a free hour between meetings. And as for Rafe..." He made a scoffing noise that said it all.

"Yeah," Angie agreed, and in the ensuing silence—as they both contemplated the unlikely image of Rafe, the consummate playboy, choosing one woman for the job—it almost felt like the old Angie sitting at his side, driving him bonkers one minute, completely in accord the next. "Why do you think he made this stipulation? Your father, I mean."

"For Mau."

She contemplated that for a moment. "He knows you guys would do anything for Maura—that's a given—but he had to know she wouldn't want some token grandchild. That she wouldn't be happy unless you all were happy, not forced into it by a clause in his will."

"Yeah, but she's not to know anything about it. That's why Konrads wanted to see us alone."

"Good luck with that!" She cut him a look, part thoughtful, part rueful. "Although I do think he was pretty smart. I mean, what surer way to distract you all from mourning him?"

Tomas turned sharply, stared at her for a minute. Trust Angie to come up with that angle.

"Smart?" he wondered out loud, thinking words like contrived and cunning where closer to the truth.

Wasn't it their right to mourn a father who'd done so much for them, been so much to them?

"It worked, didn't it?" she asked.

Hell, yes. They'd barely had time to bury him before Jack Konrads called that meeting in the library and turned their sorrow into anger.

Tomas shook his head, dismissing the whole topic with a gesture of impatience. "His reasoning doesn't change what we have to do."

Angie's silent regard, serious and thoughtful, tugged the bands of frustration in his chest tighter.

"What?" he barked.

"Rafe says you're not…seeing…anyone."

Her midsentence pause was just long enough for Tomas to know his brother had used another doing word. "What the hell would Rafe know about who I'm…*seeing?*"

For possibly the first time in her life, Angie's gaze dropped away from his. Probably because of his brutal emphasis on that verb. Fine. He didn't want to discuss his sex life, with her, with Rafe, with anyone.

Worse, he hated the notion that they'd been discussing it in his absence.

"Okay," she said on an exhalation. "So, do you have any sort of a plan? Other than that crazy idea of paying someone?"

"What's so crazy about it?"

"Yeesh, Tomas, do you really want that kind of woman to mother your child?"

"What kind would that be?"

She rolled her eyes. "The kind who'd do it for money."

"I'm not talking prostitution."

"Really?"

Something about her tone—and the arch of her brows—chafed his simmering frustration. "You got any better ideas? Women aren't about to line up to have my baby."

"You are so without a clue. I mean, look at you!" And

she did. She leaned back and looked at him with a narrow-eyed thoroughness that reminded him all over again how much she'd changed. "Women find that whole rugged loner thing a complete turn-on."

"What a load of bull!"

She made an impatient tsking sound with her tongue. "You get to the city occasionally…or at least you used to. You have to feel women looking you over. You can't *not* know you're like their living, breathing, outback fantasy."

Fantasy? Big deal. What he needed was reality, female and available.

"Name me one of these women," he said roughly. "One who'd have my baby."

She blinked slowly and edged back another inch. Which is when he noticed that he'd gotten right in her face. Close enough that he heard the faint hiss of her indrawn breath. The only sound in the intense silence, until she spoke.

"I would."

Two

Angie listened to those two short, stunning syllables echoing inside her head. *I would.* Where had that come from? Was she insane?

Definitely.

Otherwise she would be laughing, right? Not loopy, they're-coming-to-take-me-away-ha-ha laughter, but a smooth chuckle as she nudged Tomas and said, "Ha, ha. Got you a good one, didn't I?" Or something similarly off-hand and flippant.

Anything to fill the awkward silence and the fact that her heart was thudding so hard it physically hurt, and that she really, really wanted to confess the truth.

Well, here's the thing, Tomas....

I've loved you in some way pretty much all of my life. I've wanted to marry you ever since I was thirteen. Somewhere around fourteen I'd already named our babies—three of them, all boys, all with your baby blues.

Except she couldn't admit that. She wanted to shove the intensity of her teenage crush back in the past where it belonged. She'd come down here to try and *save* their friendship, not to send it on a headlong plummet into disaster.

Angie swallowed, and wished that his gaze hadn't dropped to her throat at that exact second. Her throat felt tight, her smile even tighter. "I've really weirded you out, haven't I?"

"Yup." He shook his head, looked away, then back at her. "Was that your intention?"

"No."

"Then…why?"

She wished she could laugh it off, but she looked into his stunned blue eyes and she couldn't laugh and she couldn't lie. All she could find was some small version of the truth. "Damned if I know, but I have to tell you that your response is not very flattering. I mean, would it be so bad? You and me?"

She felt him staring, felt the puzzlement in his sharp regard take on another flavor. Was he actually contemplating the reality? Him with her, skin to skin, doing what was necessary to make babies? Her heart skipped. The tightness in her throat and her skin took on a new dimension, a new heat.

"You can't have thought about it," he said slowly, "at all!"

Oh, how wrong could one person be. Angie had thought about it—specifically, about her and Tomas doing *it*—ever since her first sex education lesson. "Actually I have thought about it quite a bit," she said slowly. "The sex part, I mean, not the having-a-baby part."

In the midnight quiet his expulsion of breath sounded almost explosive. Apparently the concept of Sex-with-Angie was so appalling that he couldn't even look her in the eye when he told her so. He jumped to his feet and stalked to the sandstone wall at the back of the rock ledge.

Turning on his boot heels, he stared at her, all hard, shocked, affronted male. "Hell, Angie, you can't be serious. You're like…you're…"

"So unappealing you couldn't bring yourself to sleep with me? Even to keep Kameruka Downs?"

"Don't put words in my mouth. You don't know what I'm thinking," he said tightly.

No, she didn't, and between the tricky dark and the distance he'd put between them, she couldn't tell a thing from his expression. And, dammit, she wasn't about to lose her oldest friend, her pride, *and* get a cricked neck out of this.

She stood and brushed the gritty sand from the back of her dress as she closed the distance between them. *Moment of truth, sister.* "Why don't you tell me then? Why has the idea of me offering to have your baby got you so wound up?"

"Christ, Angie, we're not doing some hypothetical here. We're talking about a real situation. I need a baby." Chin jutted, he started down at her, his whole expression carved as hard as the rock at this back. Possibly harder. "A baby the mother would have to raise on her own."

Hands on hips she narrowed her gaze and stared back at him. Surely she'd heard him wrong. "Are you saying you wouldn't want any part in this child's upbringing?"

"You got it."

"But why?" She shook her head. Huffed out a breath and waved her hand at their surroundings. "You have this fabulous place for a child to grow up, and—"

"Not everyone thinks it's so fabulous."

"Well, I do! And your father obviously thought so, too, since he chose to bring you all up here. Do you think, when he drafted that clause, that he wanted you to just sire some anonymous—"

"I don't care what he thought."

"Really? Then you *have* changed."

"You've got that right, too!"

For a moment they stood toe to toe glaring at each other, until Angie realized that his expression wasn't so much tight and flat as schooled. To hide his frustration, his anger, his pain? Perhaps even his fear that if he and his brothers failed to satisfy the will stipulation, he would lose this home and career and life that he loved, right on top of losing his wife and his father.

That knowledge caught in her chest, a thick ache of sympathy and shared pain and her own dawning realization: she wasn't anywhere near to closing down this part of her past. Because for all that had changed in him, in her, in both their worlds during the last five years, one thing remained the same.

She still loved this man enough to do just about anything to ease his hurt.

Tears misted her eyes as she lifted a hand to touch the side of his face, blurring his features but not his rejection.

Both hands raised in a stop-right-there gesture, he reared back. "Forget it, Angie. Forget the pity and forget this whole crazy conversation!"

Angie's hand dropped away. Okay. She could do this. She could shrug and pretend indifference while her face and her throat and her heart ached with the effort. Restraint—in words, in actions, in emotions—did not come easily or naturally, but she sensed that now was the time to exercise some self-control.

"I care too much to forget about it," she said, slowly backing away, giving him the space he demanded, "so let's talk this through. What are your alternatives? Say you do find a woman willing to have your baby for money. Unprotected sex with a stranger is a big risk, don't you think?

"Unless you're thinking of artificial insemination, which is worth consideration," she continued, thinking on her feet, literally. "On the plus side, you get all the health checks and no awkward intimacy…I gather that is a plus, right?"

A muscle in his cheek jumped. Which probably meant he neither wanted intimacy nor wanted to talk about it. Tough. He'd stopped her leaving earlier, when she'd been ready to walk away, and now she *was* going to talk this through.

"But that all takes time, the checks and tests and the getting an appointment and such, when you don't have much leeway. Three months to conceive, right?" Angie winced. "That is not a lot of time. Especially since the conception rate would be lower."

"Why lower? A.I. works fine in cattle."

Trust Tomas, the consummate cattleman, to equate this to livestock!

Angie lifted her shoulders and let them drop in an exaggerated shrug. "How would I know? It's not as if I've actually investigated the process. I just read about it somewhere. I was trying to help you work through the possibilities is all."

"You sure you don't want to make the decision for me?"

"You've never once taken my advice on anything, why would you start now?"

"That's never stopped you offering it."

Did he mean her previous advice? About not rushing into marriage with Brooke? She stared back at him, found the answer in the grim blue hostility of his gaze. Yep, that's what he meant all right.

"I thought you wanted to talk this through," she said, finally accepting the futility of the conversation. Same old story, really. "You'd do better talking to the cliff face there. At least it won't tell you anything you don't want to hear!"

He started to say something. Judging by the look in his eyes and the hands-on-hips aggressiveness of his stance it was neither pretty nor appeasing, so Angie cut him off.

"I offered to help you, Tomas. Your answer: 'forget this whole crazy conversation.' Well, perhaps that is the best advice that's been tossed out here tonight!" She lifted a hand, part frustration, part farewell. "I'll say goodbye in the morning. When I'm not feeling so inclined to slug you."

Jaw clenched and silent, Tomas watched her disappear into the darkness from whence she'd come. He hadn't meant to hark back to the last time they'd stood toe to toe at this same waterhole. The last time she'd offered advice that he didn't want to hear.

I know you think you love her, T.J., but don't rush into marriage. Not unless you're very, very certain Brooke can handle living out here.

Yup, he'd ignored that advice and they'd both suffered the consequences, he and Brooke. Through three roller-coaster years of passion and conflict, of separations and loneliness, of stand-up fights and emotional making-up. Three years that ended in the mother of all fights and no chance to make it up, not once Brooke was gone.

He had no interest in finding another woman, but he did need to satisfy the terms of his father's will. For his mother, for Kameruka Downs, for his brothers, for himself. All he had to do was find the woman who'd do it *his* way.

That woman was not Angie. No way. She was too used to dancing to her own wild, unscored tune. Unpredictability was the only predictable thing about her. Even her off-the-cuff "I would" offer to have his baby shouldn't have floored him as it had done.

Angie had been pulling I-didn't-think-this-through stunts all her life.

No, it wasn't so much the offer that had rendered him speechless as the disturbing stuff that went hand-in-hand. She'd thought about having sex with him. *Quite a bit,* she'd said.

Sensations burned through his blood, images burned into his brain, and with a low growl of frustration he flung his body at the path and attacked the climb back to the homestead.

That wasn't going to happen. Not with Angie. He wouldn't allow himself to think of her in those terms. Not naked, not in his bed, not beneath his body.

No, no, absolutely no.

She hadn't meant she would, really, have his baby. Only hypothetically. And even if she had meant it, she would soon change her mind. A woman who couldn't settle in one place—in one job—for longer than a month or three wasn't going to cut it as a mother. Sure, she'd changed. She'd grown up some, but she hadn't yet settled down. He didn't know if her gypsy heart ever would.

Back at the homestead he found Rafe lurking in the shadows by the door. An ambush, he suspected. If he hadn't been so preoccupied by the worrying exchange with Angie, he might have suspected as much and avoided it.

"Alex gone to bed?" he asked, stepping onto the veranda.

"He's on the phone. Business continues."

Even past midnight on the night of his father's funeral. That was Alex.

Rafe lifted his liqueur glass. "Care to join me in a nightcap?"

"Another time."

But when he reached for the door, Rafe sidestepped to block his way. So neatly and pseudo-casually that Tomas knew it was no accident. "Don't suppose you happened across Ange out there in the dark?"

Trick question. Tomas's whole body tensed although he schooled his face into passive indifference. Either Rafe had already seen her coming in—had maybe even talked to her—or she'd snuck under his radar by using the side entrance. "Isn't she inside?"

"She wasn't in her room when I checked a while back."

Tomas crossed his arms. Said nothing, gave away nothing. He suspected Rafe would fill him in on why he was looking for Angie without any prompting on his behalf.

"I had this notion, y'see, about the will." Lips pursed, Rafe swirled the liquid in his glass. Tokay. The same dark amber as Angie's eyes. The same eddying whirlpool as in Tomas's gut as he waited for Rafe to continue. "I think Angie's the answer."

"This isn't her problem," Tomas said tightly. "Leave her out of it."

"She knows the whole story so no tricky explanations are necessary. And Mau loves her like a daughter already."

And there was the problem. Angie and her brothers had grown up like part of the family. Their father had cooked for the Carlisles—he'd moved out to Kameruka Downs after his wife died, head-hunted by Chas because he'd cooked at Maura's favorite Sydney restaurant. The Moris had occupied one of the workers' cottages but the kids had spent as much time in the homestead as their father. The six of them, Carlisles and Moris, had grown up together, played together, been schooled together.

"From where I'm standing," Rafe continued, "Angie's the perfect solution."

"From where I'm standing, she's too much like one of the family."

"You mean like our sister?" Surprise whistled out on Rafe's exhalation. "Can't say I feel the same way, not since she's come back from Italy with the new haircut and that body and the walk." Rafe eyed him a moment. "You did notice the walk?"

The sexy sway of her hips? The gauzy skirt that clung to her legs? The glint of a gold ankle chain against smooth olive skin? "No."

"The sad thing is I believe you." Rafe shook his head, his expression a studied mix of disgust and pity. He sipped from his drink, then narrowed his eyes. "Although this does make things less complicated."

"How's that?"

"No need to toss you for her."

Tomas frowned. "I don't follow…."

"Ange is the perfect solution for one of us. If you're not interested, then I'll ask her."

To sleep with *him,* to have *his* baby? Tomas was shaking his head before the thought finished forming. "You and Angie? No way."

"Why not?"

Tomas forced himself to relax. His fingers, he realized, had curled into fists. His gut felt about the same. "What makes you think she'd be interested in helping either one of us out?"

"She has this thing about owing the family. For Mau looking out for her with all the girl stuff and Dad getting her into the fancy boarding school. For keeping her father on the payroll even after he was too sick to work."

"That's bullshit." Not what the Carlisles had done for Joe Mori and his family—that was all true—but the debt thing. "She doesn't owe us a thing."

"She thinks she does."

"You're not serious. About asking her to…" Tomas couldn't say the words. They stuck in his throat, all wrong.

"There isn't anyone I'd rather ask."

"I thought you didn't give a damn about your inheritance."

"I don't." Rafe swallowed the rest of his drink, then clamped a hand on Tomas's shoulder. Their eyes met and held, his brother's intensely serious for once. "But I know how much you care about yours."

"You're not martyring yourself for me."

"One in, all in. Your words, little brother, and the only way to do this thing. We increase our chance of success and lessen the onus on any one of us. No martyrs here, Tomas, just realists out to get the job done."

"Not with Angie," he said tightly.

"Think about it, bro'. She is just about perfect." And with a last squeeze of his shoulder, Rafe turned and disappeared into the house.

The motionless silhouette of horse and rider etched against the clear blue sky must have been a mirage, because when Angie lifted a hand to shield her eyes from the morning sun, only a single Leichardt pine broke the horizon. She sat forward in the passenger seat and stared harder through the Land Rover's dusty windscreen.

Right the first time—nothing broke the mile-long line of ridge save that tree. The crazy woman not only let fly with impulsive offers in the midnight dark, but now she'd started seeing things! With a rueful half laugh, she sank back into her seat. And heard the driver clear his throat.

"You all right, mate?"

"Fine," she assured Jeremy, the stockman who'd been coopted into driving her to the airstrip. "I thought I saw someone up on the ridge is all."

"Coulda been the boss."

"Oh?" Angie forced herself to sound casual. "He's out riding then?"

"Went out at sunup. Coulda been him up there."

Good to know she wasn't delusional. Not so good to know that Tomas had ridden out at dawn, was likely somewhere beyond the Barakoolie ridge right now, and therefore stood no chance of arriving at the airstrip before they left for Sydney.

Disappointment spiked, quick and sharp, in her chest. She shook her head. What had she expected? A chance to say goodbye or a last second I've-been-thinking-about-what-you-said-last-night turnaround?

Is that what she even wanted?

After a night spent tossing and turning, she'd thought not. Sometime in the hour before dawn she'd managed to talk herself into a rational, sensible acceptance that she had no business offering Tomas anything.

So, okay, she had felt rudderless in the last months, unsure what she wanted to do with her life, where she wanted to live, how she wanted to live. She'd returned to Australia because Charles Carlisle was dying, but now she knew she was home to stay.

But having a baby, even Tomas's baby…

In perfect synchronicity with her heart and stomach, the Land Rover lurched and bounced through a series of potholes.

"That snuck up on me, mate. Sorry."

Jeremy, barely seventeen and a hoon at heart, grinned unapologetically without slowing down. In fact, he applied a tad more gas as he swung the vehicle in a wide circle before skidding to a dusty stop alongside the plane. Angie tsked her disapproval although she'd driven in much the same way growing up here.

As she slid down from the cab her gaze skimmed along the empty horizon one last time. She called the resultant hollow sensation deep inside hunger. After all that tossing and turning and self-debating, she had slept eventually. Right through her alarm.

Meaning Rafe had turfed her out of bed with no time for anything but a hasty shower and a quick farewell to Maura and the household staff. Too late to catch a lift when the boys left to perform their pre-flight checks. Too late for breakfast.

She ferreted a fruit bar from her bag and wrinkled her nose in disgust. "I don't suppose you've got anything less healthy on you?" she asked Jeremy as they walked side by side to the plane.

"Nah. Sorry, mate."

"Too bad." While Jeremy stowed her luggage she finished the breakfast substitute, but the hollow feeling in her stomach only intensified. "Do you suppose they're almost ready for takeoff?"

"Just about."

For some reason Angie wasn't. She'd come up north for the funeral, but also to say farewell to her childhood home and her teenage daydreams. Instead she felt…fretful.

As if she were leaving something behind, unfinished.

"See ya later then, Ange."

With a casual wave, Jeremy started to turn away and ridiculous panicky I'm-not-ready-to-leave tears sprang to Angie's eyes. Before she could stop herself she grabbed hold of the young jackaroo and planted a smacker on his cheek.

So, okay, the kid looked a dozen shades of embarrassed as he sidled away, but *she* felt better. She even managed a big smile as she called after him, "Look after yourself. And drive carefully."

Holy cow. She sounded like a mother!

Was that some kind of a sign? Her destiny sneaking up to answer all the unanswered questions of the night?

Smile fading, she let her hand drop away from its cheerful wave as the ute sped off, dust billowing in its wake. She didn't know if this atypical fragility stemmed from returning home after so long away, the emotional circumstances of her visit, or lack of sleep.

Most likely, all of the above.

With a hitch of one shoulder, she started up the steps of the plane. The engines turned over with a high-pitched whine, and a sudden gust of wind plastered her skirt to her legs and tangled her shoulder-length hair. Pausing to rake the thick tresses back from her face, she felt compelled to take one last look over her shoulder.

Her attention snagged on a distant spurt of movement. Not the rapidly departing Jeremy and not an illusion, either.

A horse and rider loped steadily across the treeless flats, heading straight toward the airstrip.

Three

Angie pressed the palm of one hand flat against her chest. "Steady up there," she cautioned her heart which had taken off at a wild gallop. *Even if it is Tomas, he's likely just coming to see us off or to deliver a last minute message to his brothers.*

Or something.

Rafe called out to her from inside the plane, hurrying her along. Alex, she knew, was already in the pilot's seat. She waved a stalling hand, her eyes fixed on the approaching rider. No one sat a horse quite like Tomas. The familiarity of that sight and the knowledge that she *would* get to say goodbye, soothed the ragged rawness of her emotions. Her pulse, however, continued to race as she watched him dismount and start toward her, not in any hurry yet still eating up the ground with his easy, long-legged stride.

No one wore a pair of Wranglers quite like Tomas.

Those work-worn jeans and the dusty roper boots beneath came to a halt at the foot of the stairs. Two steps up, Angie held a height advantage for the first time in her life and she felt a renewed surge of emotion.

This time it was *good* emotion, as strong and dazzling as the northern sun. Leaning down, she tipped back the tan Akubra that shadowed his face from the bright rays of that morning sun.

"You almost missed us," she said.

"Damn straight he did." Rafe, curse his timing, leaned out the aircraft door and broke their second of eye-meet connection. "Nice of you to drop by and see us off, bro'."

"Wanted to make sure you were leaving, bro'."

Rafe chuckled and Angie couldn't suppress a grin at the dry banter. It was so typical, so familiar, so brotherly. Then Tomas's serious gaze shifted back to hers and froze the amusement on her lips. "And I wanted to see Angie."

"Don't keep her too long," Rafe warned. "Alex is itching to get back to work."

He left them alone then, she and Tomas and the memory of their last conversation stretching tense and awkward in the ensuing silence. Angie's nerves twitched impatiently.

"If this is about what I said last night—"

"I've been thinking about what you said—"

They both spoke at the same time; both stopped at the same time. Their eyes met and locked and Angie felt a curious breathlessness. "You first," she managed to murmur. "Go ahead."

"When you said you would—hypothetically—have this baby, was the offer…exclusive?"

What?

Angie felt her spine snap straight with the implication.

"I hope you're not insinuating I would go around offering to have babies for every Tom, Dick and Harry."

His disconcerted gaze flicked toward the plane and understanding dawned, startling a cough of laughter from Angie's mouth. *Not every Tom, Dick and Harry, just every...*

"Rafe and Alex?"

He shifted his weight from one boot to the other. "Rafe seems to think you'd do this because you owe the family."

"You discussed me with Rafe?" she asked on a rising note of disbelief.

"He brought it up. He seems to think you're the perfect choice."

"And what about you, Tomas? Have you given any thought to *your* choice?"

"I've been thinking about it all night." His eyes narrowed, deepening the creases at their corners. Making those clear blue irises glint like cool water under a summer sky. Making her heart stutter and restart low in her belly. "Will you help me, Angie?"

And there it was, a simple request spoken so quietly and sincerely that it turned her inside out and upside down. Knowing how much fulfilling this will clause meant to Tomas, how could she refuse? "If I can," she said, just as softly. "Yes."

His nostrils flared a fraction. His eyes sparked with... something. "Why?"

Because you need me. Because I love you. "Because I can."

He looked away, huffed out a breath, said something low and indecipherable and probably not meant for her ears. Slowly his gaze came back to hers. "Still as impetuous as ever?"

Angie shrugged. "Apparently."

For a long moment they stood in silence, gazes locked, while Angie's heart screamed at roughly the same decibels as the plane's engines.

What are you doing? it wailed. *What are you saying?*

"What now?" she asked, knowing even as she asked what she wanted. Some sign that this was more real than it felt. That she really had just offered to have his baby. "Do you want me to stay?"

"No," he said quickly. Adamantly. Then he lifted a hand to the brim of his hat, tipping it lower on his brow so his eyes were in shadow. "I'm coming to Sydney next week. I'll make an appointment with a doctor."

"You don't need to…" Her voice trailed off as she remembered what she'd talked about, so glibly, the night before. Then it had been about some hypothetical partner with an unknown sexual history. Now it was about her and Tomas and… She drew a swift breath and lifted her chin. "Yes, we should have the tests, to make sure we're both healthy."

He stared at her a moment. "I meant a fertility center."

"Surely there's no need for that."

"There is. For insemination."

Angie's mouth fell open. "You're kidding, right?"

He wasn't. She could see that in the rigid set of his jaw, in the muscle that flexed and released in his cheek. "It's got to be artificial."

"Got to be?" Angie asked calmly, as if she weren't flailing around trying to get a grasp of something solid. "Because when you asked for my help, when I said yes, I was thinking about doing this the way nature intended."

"No," he said tightly. "That's not going to happen."

Angie fought an irrational urge to laugh or cry or scream—or perhaps not so irrational. The situation, this conversation, the stilted way they kept tiptoeing around straight language, was all too unreal. She couldn't believe how calmly she'd offered to sleep with Tomas, to make love, to try to conceive a baby.

And she couldn't have imagined how much it would hurt, seeing how fiercely he objected.

"Is the idea of sleeping with me so distasteful that you'd prefer doing it on your own? Because most men—"

"Leave it be, Angie!" He muttered a rough word, one that was fairly pertinent to the topic, Angie thought. "It won't work."

"Functionally?" She came down a step so she was right on a level with his face. So she could see the heightened color that traced his cheekbones. See the rigid line of his lips.

Hear the breath he sucked through his teeth. "I meant you and me, any way other than artificial."

"It's only sex," she fired back, her patience so close to snapping she could feel the twitch in her nerves. "Surely you could lie back, close your eyes and think of Kameruka!"

Their gazes clashed, so hot and hostile that neither noticed Rafe's reemergence from the plane until he cleared his throat. "Sorry to interrupt, folks, but we've really got to get moving."

"Two minutes." Angie didn't turn around but she held up a hand. "Just give me two minutes."

She had no clue what she would do with those precious minutes, whether she would sock Tomas one for his stubbornness or take his face between her hands and kiss him one. Just to prove that she was a woman and he was wrong and that this could work if he'd only give her a chance.

Still simmering she leaned a fraction closer, until she could see into the shadow cast by his broad-brimmed hat and beyond the hostility of his stance to the man beneath. And what she saw there sucker-punched her heart.

He looked so torn, so trapped, so tormented.

Ahh, Tomas…

Like butter under the outback sun, her own animosity melted. “I so wish you hadn’t been forced into this.”

She lifted a hand to touch his face, and for a whisper of time he allowed it. She felt the bristly texture of his unshaven cheek, the warmth of an exhaled breath, the tension that held his whole body straight and erect, and she ached to hold him, to bury her face in that hollow between shoulder and neck, to nuzzle his skin.

And she wanted to kiss him so badly that her lips stung with the wanting, but already she could feel him preparing to pull away. She didn’t give him a chance to get any further. Taking his face firmly between both hands, she ducked beneath that broad-brimmed hat and planted her lips on his.

There, Tomas Carlisle, take that.

With her eyes wide-open she saw the shock in his narrowed blue ones, felt the resistance in his stiff lips and the jolt of reaction—in him, in herself—as her mouth opened softly. Then he wrenched her hands away, turning his face so her lips grazed the corner of his mouth and across his whiskery cheek.

She was left kissing nothing but the morning air, left staring into eyes that blazed with blue fire. “You can’t stand even a kiss?” she asked.

He thumbed the hat back up his forehead, aggravation etched all over his face. “Dammit, Angie, why are you forcing this? If you’re willing to help, then why not my way?”

Because this was her chance—probably her only chance—to have him, and if she could have him and love him and give him the family he needed, then maybe she could also heal his wounded heart. She didn’t know if that was possible, but she had to take a chance. One thing she did know for sure and certain—if she told him how she felt, she wouldn't see his Wrangler-wrapped backside for swirling black bulldust.

So she rocked back on her heels, folded her arms across her chest, and shrugged. "If I'm going to sacrifice myself to have this baby, I'm not going to be dudded out of all the fun."

For maybe half a second he went completely still—as if she'd *really* shocked him—and then he shoved his hat low on his forehead and took a slow step backward. Then another. "This is business, Angie, not fun."

"And business can't be fun?"

"Not anymore," he said tightly. And he turned and strode away.

"Nice work, Ange," Rafe drawled from behind her.

She didn't turn around, she was too focused on Tomas's retreat. His broad shoulders were bunched with tension, his long legs moving as if he couldn't get far enough away from her quickly enough.

Nice work?

"Only if my job description was 'lose a good friend,'" she said softly.

Rafe's hand squeezed her shoulder, but the gesture of support and reassurance didn't do much to ease the thickness in her chest and throat. "You gave him plenty to think about for the next week, don't you think?"

She frowned back over her shoulder. "What about next week?"

"We're meeting in Sydney."

"We?"

"Alex, myself, Tomas. We're meeting with Konrads again. About the will."

Angie's gaze slid, helplessly, back to the man who now

sat still and watchful on his horse. Making sure she did leave? “Are you suggesting he might change his mind?”

“With a little help.”

“What kind of help?” she asked suspiciously.

“Last night I mentioned asking you to help *me* out. My little brother objected rather strenuously.”

“*I* object rather strenuously!”

Rafe winked. “Yeah, but he doesn’t need to know that.”

“What are you suggesting?”

“A little competition wouldn’t harm your cause, babe.”

Yes, the Carlisles hated to be outdone, especially by each other. Hadn’t Tomas’s first words this morning been about her offering herself to the wider Carlisle cause? Angie’s gaze shifted back to the motionless rider and her heart skipped a half-beat.

“Between that and what you’ve given him to think about…”

“What’s that?” she asked.

“Close your eyes, lie back, and think of Kameruka.” Rafe grinned and shook his head. “Nice work, Ange.”

“Have either of you considered other methods?” Tomas felt the impact of his brothers’ undivided attention before he looked up from his plate and found them both staring at him, obviously baffled by his out-of-the-blue question.

Around them the late-lunch activity continued in the restaurant of the Sydney Carlisle Grande Hotel. Patrons ate. Waiters waited. Tomas didn’t notice.

He didn’t recall eating his meal. Didn’t recall what they’d discussed while they ate. His attention had been fixed solely on the outcome of their prelunch meeting with Jack Konrads, a week to the day after they’d last met in the Kameruka Downs library.

Long story short: they could fight their father's will. But then they would have to live with the knowledge that they'd disrespected his last wish.

They had to do this. They had to try.

"Other methods—" Rafe rocked back in his chair "—of eating? Meeting?"

"The baby," Tomas elucidated. "Artificial conception. I'm thinking of going to a—" Center? Service? Frowning, he searched for the right term. "What do you call those places?"

"A breeding farm?" Rafe suggested.

"A clinic." Alex put his cutlery down and fixed Tomas with a steely look. The kind he used often in the boardroom to show he meant business. "You don't have to do this—either of you. That message I got before…"

Vaguely Tomas recalled Alex's phone blipping just as their meals arrived.

"Susannah has agreed to marry me."

There was a moment of shocked silence, broken when a waiter arrived to remove their plates. Rafe recovered first and gestured toward the phone. "Are you saying Susannah agreed to marry you by *text message?*"

"She knows we're on a short timeline. I told her I wanted to know as soon as she reached a decision."

Rafe shook his head sadly. "And they say romance is dead."

For once Tomas was in complete agreement with Rafe. Sure, his eldest brother kept a brutal work schedule. Susannah, too, ran her own business. But, still…

"Aren't you going to congratulate me?" Alex asked.

"Only if you can manage to look slightly happy about it," Rafe replied at the same time as Tomas said, "You're only marrying because of the will."

And in his opinion, that just sucked cane toads. A marriage wasn't a business transaction. It was about love and partnership and commitment.

Till death us do part.

"Ah, hell." He didn't realize he'd been screwing up his napkin until he threw the tightly wadded missile onto the table and rolled the crystal salt shaker. "You don't have to marry her, Alex."

"Yes. I do." Alex folded his napkin in half and half again. Placed it neatly on the table. "That's the only way I'll do this."

"When's the wedding?" Rafe asked.

"There's the mandatory thirty-day wait, but as soon as possible. We haven't decided where."

"Not at home?" Rafe asked "Mau will want to be there." By home he meant Kameruka Downs, where they'd all grown up and where Tomas still lived. Their mother, too, in her own place built after his marriage. She rarely left her remote outback home these days. Since intense media scrutiny had led to a breakdown after she'd lost her fourth child to SIDS, she despised the city, crowds, photographers.

"We're negotiating," Alex said. "Susannah has family interstate."

"Not wanting to get personal," Rafe said carefully. "But does Susannah know she's expected to, um, produce an heir right off the bat?"

"She knows." Alex checked his watch, frowned. "I have a meeting to get to, but I wanted you both to know I've got this covered."

Rafe and Tomas exchanged a look.

"You've got your part of the deal covered," Rafe corrected.

"We'll look after ours," Tomas added. "One in, all in." He got to his feet at the same time as his brothers, and offered his hand. "Congratulations, Alex. I hope it works out for you."

There was a moment, a connection that extended far beyond the firm handshake, the quick slap on the back, even the strong meeting of sky-blue eyes. It was the bond of brothers, the knowledge that a pact made would never be broken. They were all in this together, and, come hell or high water, they would make it work.

Then Alex was striding off between the tables with his trademark sense of purpose. Standing side by side, his brothers watched him out the door before Rafe shook his head. "Do you suppose he proposed by text or e-mail or intercompany memo?"

"Wondered the same thing myself." Tomas scrubbed a hand over his face. "It's not that I don't like Susannah, it's just that she's…Susannah."

Not Susie, like Angelina was Angie, but always the whole three syllables. Always so formal and cool and dispassionate. So absolutely unlike Angie.

"The whole deal's too cold-blooded and impersonal," he said, and he felt Rafe's gaze switch and focus on his face.

"As cold-blooded and impersonal as artificial conception?"

"That's different."

"I won't dignify that with a response." Rafe shook his head and indicated the door. "You ready to go?"

Nothing more was said—and that surprised the hell out of Tomas—until they were out in the lobby and about to part ways. "Did you know Ange is working here?" Rafe asked conversationally.

Tomas tensed, then covered quickly by casting a casual glance back at the restaurant. "Waitressing?"

"I meant here as in the Carlisle Grande, in my office.

She asked if I had any jobs going last week, flying home from your place, after—"

Rafe made an expansive gesture and Tomas thought, *Yeah, after.* That about summed it up.

"I gather you're not even considering her offer?"

No longer casual, Tomas's gaze cut back to his brother's face. "She told you about that?"

"We talked some. I've seen a fair bit of Ange this last week."

What the hell did "talked some" mean? And "seen a fair bit of"? Was that in the office or out of hours?

Tomas forced his fingers to unfurl out of fists. Forced himself to ask some other question, any other question. "What are you going to do about the baby?"

"I have some prospects."

"Angie?" he asked before he could stop himself.

"She's one." Lips pursed, Rafe studied him narrowly. "That won't be a problem, now you've decided to go elsewhere?"

"If it's a problem," Tomas said shortly, "it's not mine."

What else could he say? How could he object? He shook hands and watched Rafe walk away. His own decision was made and it involved a clinic and a nameless faceless woman he had to somehow find. It didn't involve any kind of passion or emotion or commitment. It sure as hell didn't involve Angie's boldly stated way of doing things!

Close your eyes, lie back, and think of Kameruka.

How many times had he closed his eyes this last week, lying back in the restless tangle of his sheets, and thought about Angie? Her soft lips grazing his skin, her exotic perfume adrift in his blood, her dark eyes filled with the wild promise of passion as she came to him in the dark.

It's only sex.

If only he could believe that. If only he could get past the disturbing notion of the action and cut straight to the result. Because he could imagine Angie with a baby, in a wildly sensuous earth-mother way.

But Rafe's baby?

The notion burned his gut like battery acid, the wrongness and the certainty that if his brother asked, Angie would say yes. Women didn't say no to Rafe. Ever.

Ah, hell.

Instead of heading out to the street on a quest for cold and impersonal, he found himself in an elevator going up to the executive floor of the Carlisle Grande Hotel. And his gut burned worse than ever.

Four

He found her office empty, yet Tomas had no doubt that this was Angie's workspace. Less than two days on the job—not enough time to even change the name-plate on the door—and already she'd stamped her personality all over the place. Some—Alex came to mind—would call her desk a disaster. She would shrug and call it work in progress.

Knowing Angie, that would mean at least a dozen pieces of work in simultaneous progress.

Amid all the open folders and scattered paperwork sat a bright blue coffee mug which he knew wouldn't be empty. Angie rarely finished anything in one sitting. Relaxing a notch, he strolled over to the desk and checked. Yup, the mug was still half full.

Wry amusement twitched at the corners of his mouth as he straightened. His nose twitched at the scent of her perfume...or perhaps that was the bunch flowers shoved higgledy-piggledy into a red glass jar. She had a framed collage of pictures, too. One of her parents smiling into each other's eyes on their wedding day, a more recent picture of her father gaunt with the illness that took his life, and a candid shot of the three Mori kids goofing off at the Kameruka Downs waterhole.

He'd probably been there that day—for all he knew, he could have taken the picture. There'd been so many days like that back then.

But what about now?

Tomas put the frame back, next to the coffee mug, amid the chaos that was Angie's workspace. She'd taken a convenient job here with Rafe, but how long did she intend staying? Was she ready to settle down? Enough to raise a baby?

His mood had turned grim long before his thumb brushed over the rim of the mug, smudging the glossy imprint of her lipstick.

This was the Angie of now, the woman he didn't know.

The one who stained her lips the color of mocha, whose lips had imprinted his with the fleeting taste of temptation. The one whose velvet-brown eyes spoke of another wildness, a different type of passion to the laughing girl in the waterhole picture. *This* was the woman who'd stood on the steps of the plane and calmly suggested that sex between them could be fun.

With a silent oath he jerked away from the desk, his action so abrupt he almost upset the mug. He righted it quickly, pushing aside papers to make some space. And that's when he found the book.

Babies Made Easy.

He was still staring at the cover, bemused by her choice

of reading material and the irony of that title, when Angie returned.

He heard the quick approach of footsteps in the corridor and sensed her hesitation in the doorway, her presence licking through him like the memory of her kiss—a sweet suggestion of heat and anticipation, chased away by instant hostility. Not toward Angie herself, but toward the unwanted response of his body. He didn't know how to handle this new awareness, the strange tug in his gut, the tight dryness in his throat.

Because she was standing there watching him, eating him up with those big brown eyes.

"I didn't expect to find you here." She came into the room then, smiling with a warmth that made him think she didn't mind the surprise. "How did the meeting go?"

Of course she knew they'd been meeting with the lawyer. Rafe would have told her. They talked a lot, after all. "A waste of everyone's time," he said curtly, irritated that the thought of her and Rafe doing anything together completely wiped away the effect of her smile.

"There's no way out of the clause?"

"None we're prepared to take."

"So, you have to make a baby." Not a question but a matter-of-fact statement as she leaned her hips against the desk at his side. She looked like a candidate for Ms. Hotel Management, in her crisp white shirt and knee-length black skirt, her hair sleek and neat, her only jewelry a fine gold neck-chain bearing the letter A.

At least she was smiling her usual Angie smile, warm and relaxed and spiced with a dash of wryness.

Then she noticed the book in his hand and her smile faltered. His appreciation of that smile nosedived right alongside. He tapped a finger against the book's cover, right under the title. “Interesting choice of reading, Angie.”

“I thought I’d research the topic, in case I needed to help any friends out.”

“Friends like Rafe?”

“Like Rafe or Alex or Tomas,” she corrected without hesitation. “It’s fascinating reading…although I have to say the title is very misleading.”

No kidding.

“Did you know there’s only a seventeen percent chance of conceiving each month? With odds like that, you need to get started. You all do!”

“That’s why I’m here.”

Their eyes met and held for a second, and he sensed a stillness in her, a new intensity beneath her aura of casual confidence, as if he’d surprised the breath right out of her. Hell, he’d surprised himself even though the words had come out of his mouth!

“Have you changed your mind?” she asked.

“Have you?” he countered.

“About making a baby in some sterile clinic?” With a glancing brush of fingers, she took the book from him and tossed it onto the desk. “Absolutely not.”

“I meant about helping me.”

“Does it matter? Since we don’t see eye to eye on the method, my offer of help is moot.”

“Maybe we can compromise. About the method.”

“Really?” Eyebrows arched, she regarded him steadily for a drawn-out second. “How would that work, do you suppose?”

Tomas shifted uncomfortably. He didn’t have an answer. Until this last minute he hadn’t fixed on what he’d hoped to achieve by coming up here. Making sure she didn't get tangled with his hound of a brother, yeah, but as for how—

"Yeesh, Tomas." She interrupted his thoughts with obvious irritation. "You don't know why you're here, do you? Nothing's changed from last week."

"You don't know that."

"I know that you couldn't even stand me kissing you, so why chance anything more intimate?" She blew out a short, impatient breath, and when she started to turn away Tomas reacted instinctively, stopping her retreat with a hand on her arm. For a long moment she just stood there gazing up at him, her eyes widened with surprise.

Good.

He'd caught her on the back foot for a change, and with subtle emphasis he shifted his grip on her arm, not exactly tightening but…adjusting. Just so she knew he meant to keep her there until he was done. Whatever he had to say, whyever he'd changed his mind and come upstairs, he had to put into words. Now. "You caught me by surprise last week."

"So—" she lifted her chin "—if I'd given you more notice you wouldn't have minded me kissing you?"

"I don't know."

"You don't know," she repeated softly, her gaze narrowing and darkening. "Do you want to find out? Or do you want to let go of my arm so I can get back to work?"

The challenge gleamed hot in her eyes, daring him to make that choice. *It's only a kiss,* he told himself, but that phrasing didn't help. Not when her words from last week twined sinuously through his consciousness.

It's only sex.

And this was a test. If he could kiss her, if he could just bend his head to hers and go through the motions, then maybe he could do the sex part, too. Maybe.

He heard the huff of her exasperated breath, felt her start to pull away and blocked her escape with his body. Their eyes met and held. An awareness of what they were about to do charged the air between them, but a breath away from her lips, he paused, too charged with tension to breach that final inch of space.

"Go ahead," she said softly. "I won't bite...unless you want me to."

His head reared back, dumbfounded when he should have expected no less. This was Angie, after all. Angie who was shaking her head with renewed exasperation.

"I was kidding. A joke, you know. Humor."

Yeah, he knew, he just wasn't in a kidding mood, not by a long shot.

And that she must had read on his face because she sighed, a soft relenting whisper, as she leaned forward and touched her thumb to his chin. Then she shocked the hell out of him by reaching up and kissing him there. He felt the softness of her lips, the moist warmth of her tongue and then her retreat.

A small smile hovered on her lips as she whispered, "Sorry."

Sorry for the joke? Or for striking him dumb with that one swift touch of her tongue. Tomas tried to wrap his astonishment into words, to ask what she meant, but she took his face between her hands—the same as she'd done at the plane—and looked right into his eyes, her gaze dark and steady and serious.

"That was your notice." She stretched to kiss one corner of his mouth and then the other. "I'm going to kiss you now, okay?"

Before he could begin to recover his equilibrium, she moved her lips against his with soft restraint, as if she was expecting his withdrawal…or waiting for him to take a more active role. A raw, male part of him itched to take over, but a stronger, harsher voice hammered away in resistance. It wouldn't let him forget that this was Angie, and he had no business wanting to close his eyes and immerse himself in the lush temptation of her lips.

"Relax," she whispered, her breath a shiver of sensation on his skin and in his blood. Her thumbs stroked his cheeks, down to the corners of his mouth. "It's only a kiss."

And then she kissed him the same way she tackled everything—with the same energy and heat and wholehearted passion. She kissed and she willed him to open up, to unwind, to let go. She made a sound low in her throat, a kind of smoky humming that rolled through him in one long, hot wave of desire that caught him totally unprepared, completely at a loss. All he could do was close his eyes and thread his hands into the thick softness of her hair and kiss her back.

Lord, how he kissed her back. With a hunger he couldn't control, with a thoroughness he no longer wanted to control, with a yearning for all the intimacies he'd missed in the last years.

Since Brooke died.

That thought stalled his senses, slammed at his conscience, dragged him out of the drugging depths of that hot, wet contact. Intimacy was not what he wanted. No way. This was only a trial, proof that he could close his eyes and forget himself for long enough to do what had to be done. A means to an end and that was all.

He hauled himself back into his own space and switched his expression to deadpan. Not difficult—he'd had a lot of practice in recent years. Angie had slumped back against the desk. She shook her head as if to clear it and her eyes looked a little dazed. Her hair was a wild tumble, her lips kissed naked and pliant, and when she crossed her arms under her breasts, he couldn't help but notice the outline of her nipples right through her respectable white shirt.

Heat tightened his skin, itched in his hands, swelled in his flesh. He looked away, forced himself to focus on the next step, now he'd conquered the first.

"So," she said on a breathy exhalation. "That didn't seem to go too badly."

His eyes met hers, held, didn't let go. "Do you still want to help me?"

For a long second she didn't react, and he wondered if she hadn't cottoned on to his meaning, if he needed to spell out what he was asking. Again. Then her hand drifted to her throat, and she twisted the fine chain around her index finger. Her throat moved, as if she'd swallowed. "My way?"

"Yes."

"Wow." She eyed him a moment, her expression circumspect. "That's a big step up from a kiss."

"I know that."

"And you think you can take your clothes off and climb into bed with me? That you can do—"

"I don't know, okay?" And he sure as hell didn't need her talking him through every step. He could feel the heat in his face, the tightness in his jaw, in other places he didn't want to acknowledge, and he shifted his weight from one foot to the other, rearranging his weight and the tightness and the jumble of words in his brain. "I don't know, but I want to try."

"Because you want a baby?"

"Because I *need* a baby."

"Right."

There was a sting in her tone, a darkness in her eyes,

and Tomas knew he'd blown it. He knew but he didn't have the words or the sentiment to save the situation. What could he say? He had nothing to offer, no incentive, no promises, no smooth lines. None of the weapons a man like Rafe might use. And he could no more spin her lies than he could beg for her help.

"I don't expect you to commit to this right off," he said. "Not without a trial."

"Trial sex? Is that what you're suggesting?"

"One night without any commitment. If it works, then we can talk about—" He gestured toward the discarded book on top of her desk.

"Making a baby?" She stared back at him a moment, her expression inscrutable. "All right."

All right? Tomas swallowed and stared into her eyes. She meant it. For a panicky second his world tilted and spun, as if someone had hauled the rug out from under his feet. But then she was talking, planning, asking questions, and he forced himself to focus.

"Do you want me to come home with you?" he heard through the roaring in his ears. "I could—"

"No!" Not in his home, not in his bed. "No," he repeated less stridently. "That's not necessary."

"Well, I can't invite you home to my place because I don't have a place. I'm staying with Carlo."

Her brother, his friend. God, no! "I think we should keep this quiet, just between us."

"In case it's a humiliating disaster and we can't look each other in the eye again?"

"In case it doesn't work out," he said, meeting her eyes and refusing to think about such dire consequences. "Neutral territory would be best."

"I suppose a hotel room shouldn't be too hard to organize, given your family owns a whole chain." Despite that wry observation, her eyes remained dark and serious. Slowly she moistened her lips. "When do you want to conduct this…trial?"

"I'm not sure when I can get away."

"You're away now," she pointed out, crossing her arms under her breasts again. Tomas forced himself to concentrate on her words. Not her body. Not the disquieting notion that he'd never seen her naked, but soon would. And he felt the rug start to shift beneath his feet again.

"The kiss worked here and now, with only a little notice," she said with the same matter-of-fact logic. "Why not this, too?"

With a long slow stroke of her hands down her thighs, she straightened her skirt and walked around her desk. "I guess you'd planned to stay overnight?"

Tomas nodded and she picked up the phone and started dialing.

"With Alex or do you have a room booked?"

"A room. Here," he managed. His throat was tight, his mouth dry, and that damn rug was moving way too fast.

"Hello, reception?" She greeted the voice on the end of the phone with a smile. "Hi, Lisa, it's Angelina Mori in Mr. Carlisle's office. You have a booking for his brother, Mr. Tomas Carlisle, for tonight? Yes? I'm looking for an upgrade if you have a suite available."

Tomas stiffened. "That's not necessary."

"The Boronia Suite is perfect," she said into the phone, ignoring both his spoken objection and the adamant shake of his head. "Yes, Lisa, only the one night. That's all Mr. Carlisle requires." Her eyes lifted to meet his, steady and direct and daring him to make something of it. "For now, at least."

* * *

Two hours later Angie was still shaking her head over how she'd hijacked the arrangements so coolly and proficiently. She hadn't let Tomas interrupt and she'd handled his objections with the same aplomb as the room upgrade.

"I've never been in a position to reserve a suite before," she told him. "If I'm going to do this, why not with style?"

And then she'd settled behind her desk, telephone receiver anchored between shoulder and ear, and mentioned how much work she needed to get done before she could meet him upstairs. A very nice ploy, beautifully stage-managed, with no room for objection. Especially when Rafe arrived at her door, his curiosity diverted by his brother's presence.

Tomas left. She shrugged off Rafe's nosiness by pretending huge interest in a bogus phone call. Really, based on the whole scene in her office from start to finish, she should have been an actress. Her talents were much wasted. Who'd have known that her heart was racing, her insides churning, her bones quivering with nervous tension?

Now, two and a bit hours later, she smiled and made small talk with a Japanese couple as the Carlisle Grande's high-speed elevator propelled her toward the upper-floor suites and her future. All in all, she felt remarkably calm. Considering she was about to have Tomas Carlisle.

Holy Henry Moses.

After she said goodbye to the couple on floor fifteen, Angie pressed an unsteady hand against her stomach, drew a deep breath, and willed everything to stop spinning. Although she hadn't decided how, she knew she could go through with this. She knew because of the kiss that still burned strong and fierce in every cell of her blood, a kiss edged with darkness and barely leashed desperation.

He didn't want her, but he *needed* her.

And if all went well, she might not only have Tomas Carlisle this once but she might get to keep him. To live with him as she grew big with his baby, to ease the haunted shadows in his eyes, to make him laugh and smile and live again. To be more than a helpmate to secure his inheritance—to be his wife and his partner.

And if it didn't work out? If this turned into the disaster she'd alluded to in her office? Then perhaps that wouldn't be all bad if it meant closure and a signal to move on.

Perhaps she might even silence the incessant heart-whisper that had stopped her committing to any other relationship, to a career or even to a place to live. The insistent whisper that she hold back a chunk of herself, to save it for this one man, this one home, this one life. Deep down she'd always hoped…and now those hopes were about to be realized.

If he hadn't changed his mind all over again.

Outside the door to his suite—*their* suite—Angie hesitated only long enough to draw a deep breath before knocking. But then she couldn't stand the waiting, the not knowing if he was inside or not. Fumbling, swearing softly at the tremor in her hand, she managed to swipe her security card through the lock. Red light. Swearing softly she tried again, her hand more steady this time.

Green light, hallelujah.

She pushed the door open and three slow paces into the entry vestibule her heart and stomach did the same free-fall as in the swiftly ascending elevator. Still, she went through the motions of checking the huge marble bathroom, the bedroom and huge closet, but nope. The whole suite stretched before her, quiet and pristine and empty.

He wasn't here.

* * *

Angie didn't assume she'd been stood up, at least not after she'd circled the whole suite several times and given his absence considerable thought. He may have changed a lot in recent years, but she couldn't picture any version of Tomas hanging around a hotel room cooling his boot heels. He'd never done inactivity well.

She checked with reception, in case he'd left a message. Then she checked every horizontal surface—a five-star suite, she discovered, had many—and came up with no sign of a note. In fact there was no indication he'd even been here, but that was no reason to get her knickers knotted.

No, really, it wasn't.

Most likely he had business to do, seeing as he came to the city so rarely these days. Or he could be downstairs in one of the hotel bars getting well and truly drunk. The Tomas she remembered didn't need Dutch courage to tackle a wild bull or a woman, but this present one—well, she just didn't know.

Cooling heels wasn't big with Angie, either, but what else could she do but wait? Tracking Tomas down wasn't an option, not when he wanted to keep this meeting (encounter? rendezvous? one-night stand?) secret. Yeesh, but she hated not knowing what to expect or even what to call whatever-this-was she'd agreed upon. Not knowing how long she might be waiting made her even more skittish, and determined to find some way of relaxing.

If she could expend some of this pent-up emotional energy then maybe she stood a chance of loosening up Tomas. That, she knew, was essential if this night was going to work out.

She ordered up a bottle of merlot. Then, on a whim, changed her order to the kind of French champagne she'd only tasted once before, at her heartbreaker of an eighteenth birthday party. Courtesy of the Carlisles, as it happened. If Tomas Carlisle was going to make her wait, then he could pay for the luxury of unwinding her nerves!

While she waited for room service to deliver her Dom Pérignon, she filled the spa and added a liberal dash of bath-oil from the complimentary basket labeled "Body Bliss." Then she stacked the stereo with music designed for relaxation. The spa occupied roughly the same space as Carlo's whole bathroom, so she figured if the music didn't work she could use up some stray nervous energy swimming laps of the monster-tub.

Midway through the champagne and chin-deep in richly scented water, Angie felt a sudden sense of…no longer being alone. Her skin tingled, lifting hairs on the back of her neck and over her forearms. Startled, she jackknifed upright and waited, perfectly still but for the wild pounding of her heart. The music masked any sound, but when the bathroom door didn't move from its half ajar position her heart rate slowly subsided.

So much for the relaxing, luxuriating experience.

She'd started to rise from the water, to reach for a bath sheet, when the music volume dipped noticeably. Instantly her pulse skipped, her exposed nipples tightened, anticipation fizzed in her blood—as happened pretty much any time Tomas Carlisle came into the picture. Not that he was exactly in the picture, but he was close enough that her body knew; her heart knew.

And as she slid back into the water's warm embrace, she wondered if her patience could hold out until he came looking for her.

Five

How long, he wondered, could a woman stay in a bath?

Teeth gritted, Tomas attempted to block out another slush of water, another image of slick olive skin, another rush of heat to his loins. For the past two or ten or twenty minutes—God knows, it felt like an eternity!—he'd wished back that second when he'd turned down the music. Her selected volume (raucous) would have shut out the constant reminders that Angie was two open doors away, wet and naked.

Yet he couldn't bring himself to cross to the bedroom, and then to the bathroom, to do what he'd come up here to do. He didn't know what he would say. He didn't know how to begin.

Hell.

He focused hard on the view beyond the window, the lights of a city not yet ready for sleep, the traffic inching toward the bridge, late workers heading home from their jobs the same as every other evening. Everything normal, routine, unchanged in their worlds while his was spinning into some unknown dimension.

And then he caught a flutter of movement, a reflection in the glass before him, and his shoulders bunched in instant reaction. She'd exited the bedroom wearing one of the hotel's white robes, and he tracked her path across the room, saw her stop, heard the rattle of ice as she lifted the bottle.

"Can I get you a glass of champagne?" she asked. "Or would you prefer something else? I imagine there's anything you want here…."

Plus a whole lot he didn't want to want, either, he thought grimly as he turned to face her. All wrapped up in a fluffy bathrobe, dark hair gathered in a tousled ponytail on top of her head, brows arched in silent query, she stood waiting for his response.

Tomas shook his head. He'd had enough to drink downstairs. Just enough to numb the edges of his fear, but not enough to lose sight of what tonight was about.

Apparently Angie had no such reservations. He watched her pour a glass from the near-empty bottle, felt himself tense even more as she padded toward him, her bare feet noiseless on the plush claret carpet. Fine gold glinted at one ankle, and as she bent to adjust the stereo volume the chain at her neck swung forward in a slow-motion arc, then back again to settle between her breasts. *A for abundant.*

"Do you mind?" she asked.

Frowning, he forced his attention away from the deep vee of her robe. Away from the exposed slope of one breast, from the disorienting speed of blood rushing south and to the swirl of classical piano notes that seemed such an unlikely Angie-choice. "I don't mind, although that doesn't sound like your kind of music."

"Relaxation therapy, along with this—" she lifted her glass in a silent salute "—and the spa. Which, I must say, was a treat and a half."

"You needed to relax?"

"A little." The corners of her mouth quirked. "Okay, more than a little. Although I figure I now have the advantage over you, in the relaxation stakes."

"That's not saying much," Tomas admitted, and their eyes met and held in a moment of shared honesty. This wasn't going to be easy—they both knew it, they both acknowledged it.

And being Angie, she also had to try to find a way to fix it. "Are you sure you don't want a drink? Or the bathroom's free and I can really, really recommend the spa. No?"

She must have gleaned that answer from his expression, because he hadn't said a word or moved a muscle. He'd just stood there, growing more tense and rigid while she strolled right up to him. Was it his imagination or did her eyes glint with wicked purpose?

"Okay, then take off your shirt."

What?

She pushed her glass into his hand and somehow wrapped his stiff fingers around the stem. Apparently because she needed to flex her fingers, then shake them, as if limbering up. *To do what?* All that southward-rushing blood congregated in very unlimber anticipation of those fingers reaching, touching, closing around him.

"If you don't want to bother with the spa—" Angie wriggled those damn fingers some more "—then how about I give you a massage?"

"That's not necessary."

"Rubbish! You look tense enough to snap and I've been told I have magic hands." Turning to leave, she cut him a trust-me look across her shoulder. "I'll just go fetch some oil from the bathroom and then—"

"No."

"No oil?"

No oil, no magic hands stroking his shoulders, no naked thighs straddling his back. "No massage. No spa. No drinks." With subtle emphasis he placed her glass on the sill at his back, right out of her reach. "That's not why we're here."

"No, but—"

"No buts."

Their eyes met, held, locked, the air charged with the knowledge of why they were here. Sex. Not for pleasure, but for a purpose. A trial. Angie's throat moved as she swallowed, and he noticed that one hand had come up to twist at the chain at her throat. "I had this notion that we might…I don't know…sit around and talk for a bit to ease the awkwardness. Maybe order up dinner and a bottle of wine."

"Are you hungry?"

"Not really."

"Then why order dinner? This isn't a date, Angie."

Her gaze darkened, maybe hurt, maybe a little shocked at the harshness of his tone. But, in typical Angie fashion, she lifted her chin and fired right back at him. "That's it then? You just want to do it?"

"Yes." That's exactly what he wanted—to do it. No fancy trimmings, no window-dressing, no talk. And, dammit, he shouldn't feel bad about wanting what they'd both agreed on, just because she was doing him the favor. Just because she was standing there twisting that chain, looking for all the world like—

"Are you nervous?"

Probably he shouldn't have barked the question, but he

couldn't contain the surly flanks of his mood. And it seemed so unlikely that confident, unflappable, in-your-face Angie could be suffering a case of the jitters.

"Of course I'm nervous," she answered. "Aren't you?"

"Why 'of course'? You said it was 'only sex.'"

Shaking her head, she released a soft breath of laughter. "Trust you to remember that!"

"You didn't mean it?"

"Of course I didn't mean it. Saying 'it's only sex' is like saying this is only a hotel room, and Dom Pérignon is only a sparkling wine, and this—" she tugged at her lapel "—is only a bathrobe."

He could have asked why in blue blazes women didn't say what they meant, but that would be like asking why the wet season followed the dry. It simply was. But Angie? He'd always thought her a straight-shooter, and what her heated words implied sent a paradoxical chill through his blood.

"Why are you here? Why did you agree to do this?"

"I told you—because I can."

"The truth, Angie." He met her eyes, held her gaze. "No bull."

Angie stared back at him, taking in the uncompromising set of his jaw, the icy chill in eyes she'd always thought of as hot summer-blue, and her stomach swam with anxiety. Everything rested on her answer…yet if she told him her expectations, her belief that she could heal his wounded heart if he only gave her the chance, she wouldn't see him for dust.

Yet she couldn't lie. Not to him and not to herself.

"Well, there is the fact I've always wanted to sleep with you," she said slowly. Truthfully. "Oh, don't look so shocked. I told you that last week, at the waterhole. When I first suggested having your baby."

"That was hypothetical."

"Maybe you thought so. I didn't. I had a crush on you as a teenager, not that you noticed, but that's the truth. Do you remember my eighteenth?"

"The party at Shardays?"

Stupid question. Of course he remembered, since he'd met Brooke that night. But he'd asked for the truth and, painful topic or not, she couldn't stop midstory. "I remember going shopping and picking out the sexiest dress I could find for that party. It was white, this real slippery fabric that clung in all the right places." She shaped her hands over her body as she talked, remembering how excited she'd been to see herself in that dress, how keen her anticipation when she walked into the nightclub. She'd been humming with it, buzzing, singing. "I picked it out thinking about you, Tomas. I had this fantasy going that you'd see me in it and that would be it."

"You had a boyfriend."

"Yes, but he was a boy." She shrugged. "You were a man."

He made a rough sound, of disbelief or rejection or both. "That was seven years ago."

"And I've always wondered what it would be like, you and me."

"You mean you and me scr—"

"Yes." She spoke over the top of him, blocking out the harsh word he'd chosen. Deliberately, she knew, to shock her.

"Because that's all it can be," he said tightly, as if he needed to drive the point home. "Only sex."

"I hear you, although I think you should know for me it's never 'only sex,' not with any man. I'm a woman, in case I need to point that out."

"You don't."

For a long moment she stared back at him, her annoyance at his stubborn stance yielding to those two little words. He'd noticed her as a woman. And he could talk until he was blue-faced about "only sex" but her heart swelled with the knowledge that it would be so much more. If he would only give her the chance. The chance she may have blown with the honesty of her confession.

Moistening her dry lips, she concentrated on what mattered to Tomas—the reason he'd agreed to "only sex" in the first place.

"You know that book I've been reading?" She waited for his nod of acknowledgment, for him to remember the title and make the mental switch from sex-with-Angie to the end result. "Well, I've read all about fertility and conception and, frankly, you couldn't get a better candidate if you advertised. My cycle is regular as a twenty-eight-day clock, which the book says is pretty rare. I've never had any gyno problems. I'm strong and I'm healthy and I'm at my prime."

"You've thought about this. You really want to have a baby?"

"Several, eventually. All perfect angels who don't cry or give their mother a minute's grief."

She smiled. He didn't. And she sensed that she'd taken this one step too far. That perhaps she should never have admitted to nerves and thus diverted his focus back at "just do it." But, with all that had been said in the interim, how could she get back to that point?

Perhaps she did need to remind him about being a woman...a naked woman who'd agreed to have sex with him.

Slowly she closed the space between them, releasing her hair so it tumbled down past her shoulders. As she came up beside him she raked a hand through the thick tresses, no longer slick and straight but rendered thick and curly by the bathroom steam. She leaned down to recover her glass from the windowsill and her arm brushed against his in a slow heated slide. And again as she straightened.

"Have to enjoy this while I can," she said, taking a long sip of champagne. Their gazes connected over the rim of her glass. "If I do fall pregnant, I'll not have the opportunity much longer."

Something shifted in his eyes, sharpening their focus to a hard glitter for a split second before he turned abruptly to stare out the window. "There'll be a lot you have to give up."

"There'll be a lot to gain."

"What about your job?"

"It's only temporary. I'm replacing somebody on maternity leave. There's a certain irony in that, don't you think?"

He didn't answer, and Angie's confidence gave a nervy little jitter. She didn't think it possible that he could look any tenser than when she'd first come out of the bathroom, but he did. Because it was time to get down to it, to just do it, and that was easier said than done.

She took another sip of champagne but all she tasted was her own anxiety. "Awkward, huh?" she said into the lengthening silence. "This. Us. Standing here wondering what to do next."

A muscle jumped in his jaw.

"How about we go into the bedroom? At least that's a first step." When he didn't answer, she turned and started to walk in that direction.

"Angie."

She whipped back around, caught him watching her in a way that made her heart thunder like a bronco let loose on the northern plains. *Heat and fear; fear and heat.*

"Don't expect too much," he said stiffly.

"I never do."

* * *

That was a straight-out lie. Seven years she'd been waiting, wondering, ever since her coming-of-age party. Tonight she had expectations, and Tomas had no one to blame but himself.

He'd asked about her nerves. He'd insisted on the truth. No bull, he'd said, and wasn't that a load of it!

Disgusted in himself, he dragged a hand through his hair. She even remembered the damn dress, when all he remembered about that night was meeting Brooke. The only woman he'd ever loved; the only woman he *would* ever love. The only woman he'd ever taken to bed.

How the hell was he going to do this? How was he going to walk through that door and take off his clothes and lay down with another woman? What in blue blazes had made him think that doing it with Angie would be easier than with a nameless, faceless stranger?

And if he wanted honest, no-bull truth between them, why hadn't he told her about his lack of sexual experience?

Jaw set, he fought to contain the icy spread of fear through his tense body. Struggled to take the first steps toward the bedroom door, left open like an invitation to sin.

Only sex, he reminded himself. Sex with a lush, sensual woman who kissed like she loved everything about the whole man-woman intimacy thing. He imagined she wouldn't be too shy to use that mouth in all manner of ways. He imagined she wouldn't be afraid to take the initiative once he walked through that door. Maybe he should just take her advice: *Lie back, close your eyes and think of Kameruka.*

How hard could that be?

About as hard as the pounding of his pulse, he thought ruefully. And like a nagging toothache it would only get worse the longer he stood here thinking about it. Better to suck up the fear and dread of the dentist's chair and march right in there and get it over with.

If he didn't think about the intimacy, if he just concentrated on the mechanics of undoing buttons and stripping off clothes, if he focused on the part of him that cried out for a woman's slick warmth in the dead of night, the part of him that was sick of his hand providing its only satisfaction, then he could do this.

As long as she didn't expect too much.

On the threshold he paused, eyes fixed on the king-size bed that half-filled the room, covers turned back to reveal an expanse of pure white sheets. Twin bedside lamps cast a pale glow that did nothing to warm the starkness of that bed or to prevent the breakout of sweat, cold and sudden on his skin.

And Angie? His gaze swept beyond the bed and found her standing in front of the dresser, stalled in the act of brushing her hair. Their eyes locked in the mirror, as she slowly lowered her arms and put down the brush. The soft clunk sounded preternaturally loud in the stillness and he realized that her music had stopped. That the silence was so intense he could hear the thick thud of his heartbeat. Too loud, too hard.

"Damn moisture," she said, turning to face him. "Once it gets a sniff of steam, I can't do a thing to contain it."

Her hair. She meant her hair. But stupidly it took him a moment to get past the reference to moisture and steam and containing it.

"I like your hair like that." His voice sounded gruff and rusty, his compliment about as stiff as his body. "The other way, this afternoon, it was too…sleek."

"Really?" She paused in smoothing the thick mass behind her ears—a pointless task since the curls sprang free as soon as her hand dropped away. "You don't think sleek is a good look?"

"Hell, no."

"You prefer the wild look then?"

"On you," he said simply and her lips tilted at the corners in the tiniest hint of a smile. That probably would have relaxed him a notch, that connection, if her gaze hadn't drifted off to the bed—that endless stretch of cold, clinical white—before slowly returning to meet his.

"I intended taking off the robe and being all laid out on the bed waiting," she said softly. "But I couldn't do it."

"You could have left the robe on."

"I could have, if being naked was a problem." Three slow steps, three thick pulses of blood in his lower body, and she stopped in front of him. "Being naked alone was."

"You want me to get undressed?"

Dark and luminous eyes lifted from his chest to his eyes. She moistened her lips. "Do you mind if I do it?"

Not if you do it real quick.

That answer lodged in his throat when her silky female knuckles grazed his abdomen. When he sucked in hard, she got a firmer grip on his shirt and pulled it free of his trousers. Before he could think *holymotherofmercy* she'd unthreaded every button and pushed the sides of his shirt apart.

Maybe it was his vision, his thoughts, his whole body that trembled…or maybe it was her hands as they slowly traversed his bare chest, grazing his nipples, fingering the thick growth of hair, tracing the line of his collarbone. With growing confidence, her palms slid over his shoulders and down his biceps in a long, slow caress that peeled his shirt away until it dropped to the floor at their feet.

"Undo my robe," she whispered, so close that her breath

sloughed over his skin and seeped into his blood. He watched her lean forward and kiss his chest. Watched her eyelids flutter shut and that sight—soft and engrossed and sensual—brought on a surge of lust so intense his knees all but buckled.

He needed something to hold on to, to ground him against the dizzying roar of heat, and he found her robe, her sash, and a simple knot that came apart in his hands. She made a husky sound of approval as the thick toweling fell open. He made a rough sound of unscripted awe as her breasts came into view.

Full, luscious female things of beauty, with wide tawny aureoles and tips that seemed to tighten and darken as he watched—and, hell, he couldn't stop watching until he feared his mouth was watering, until he had to swallow to stop from drowning. Behind his fly, his body pulsed with an ache to reach for her, to drop to his knees and draw those distended nipples into his mouth, to take her down onto the bed and bury himself without preliminary.

Except he'd be lucky to last a minute and he owed Angie better than that. Only sex, he told himself, didn't mean it had to be bad sex.

The hands that itched to shape her body lifted instead to cup her face and he leaned down to take her lips, closing his eyes to shut out the lush appeal of her body. Their thighs brushed and her nipples grazed his chest as she came up onto her toes to meet his kiss. Restless, impatient, her hands shimmied over his ribs and sides before settling against his back and drawing their bodies into perfect alignment.

Heat billowed, a furnace of desire in his chest and his thighs and everywhere in between. Especially in between. In a slow, deep sweep his tongue stroked over hers and retreated. Her complaint was a rough sound that vibrated low in her throat and her hands tightened their grip on his back, forcing him to take notice, driving him past the edge of his control.

He kissed her harder, tasting her lips, drawing on her tongue, forcing himself to ease off when he wanted to devour. *Only sex,* he told himself, *only lust,* and that was okay. It had been so long, too long, since he'd indulged his male nature. It was understandable that he should feel so primitive, so carnal, so desperate.

Especially when she met him kiss for kiss, biting at his chin when he drew back for breath, sliding her hard-tipped breasts down his chest as she dipped lower and reached for his trousers. He sucked in another quick ragged breath but that oxygen didn't make a lick of difference when she undid the waist button and started on his fly.

The accidental brush of her fingers against his erection completely zapped his synapses, and before the red-fire haze cleared she was ducking lower, her hair a dark whisper of sensation across his stomach. For one gasp of a moment he thought she was going to take him into her mouth, and in his explosive state that would have been too much, too soon.

Thinking about that hot, moist suction was damn near enough to bring him to embarrassment.

He backed away abruptly, and sat on the edge of the bed.

"Sorry." In the low light her eyes gleamed dark and hot. "I was just helping with your trousers."

The way she was looking at him didn't help a bit. Especially with his trousers. Finally he managed to extricate himself from the rest of his clothing, and she was still watching him with a powerful hungry intensity.

"I bought condoms," he managed to say, amazed that he remembered the earlier shopping expedition. "I'll get them."

Something in her eyes darkened, as if with a sense of purpose, and through the shimmering haze of lust Tomas felt a pang of misgiving.

"You could," she said, her gaze not leaving his. "Or we could leave them right where they are and try to make a baby."

Six

"According to the book, this is my prime conception time." Sure and steady and dark as the night, Angie's eyes held his. "Do you really want to waste this chance?"

Deep inside Tomas felt a keening cry of resistance. No, he couldn't do this wholly naked. *He* needed protection, a barrier in any shape or form, some sense that he could hold himself apart from the intimacy of their bodies joining.

And how will you make a baby then? How will you keep Kameruka Downs?

His heart raced erratically, sweat sheened cold on his skin, and without a word he stood and stalked from the bedroom. Halfway across the sitting room he stopped suddenly, and for one numb second he couldn't think what he was doing or why he'd come out here.

The condoms.

His gaze closed on the box he'd tossed onto the bureau

earlier, when he'd come through the door and heard the music and realized that she was here. When it really struck home that sex with Angie was going to happen.

Do you need birth control? Do you really need this bedroom session as a trial?

Obviously he wasn't going to have any trouble functionally. Obviously Angie had made up her mind about having a baby. He could get this over with now. If luck was on his side he wouldn't have to go through this feverish ordeal of wanting and not-wanting-to-want ever again.

All you have to do is go back in that bedroom, shut down your mind and follow the lead of your body. It knows what it wants. It's not having any problem with intimacy. It wants inside Angie, naked, now.

With a grim grunt of determination, he turned and followed where that leading part of his body pointed.

Several things hit him right in the face when he walked back into the bedroom. The shapeless form of her discarded robe, stark against the wine-red carpet. How the white sheets no longer looked cold and clinical, not with Angie's darkly sensual beauty spread across them. And the fact that no amount of rubber or latex or reinforced steel could have protected him from the impact of her lying there naked.

Sucker-punched, he watched her roll up onto her knees, all tumbled black hair and perfect smooth skin and wildly generous curves. Her gaze had fixed on the highly functional and grossly underprotected body part that had lead him right back to her. He felt it thicken and pulse. Saw her moisten her lips and then move on to study his empty hands.

"You couldn't find the condoms?"

"I found them." Slowly he walked to the bed. Her eyes

arrowed back for another up-close look, probably to see what he was wearing. Or not. "I left them where they were."

Heavy-lidded eyes slid up to his. Something flickered in their dark chocolate depths. "Are you sure?"

"That I left them there? Yes. That I should have? No," he admitted, honest for once.

"If that's because we haven't talked about STDs and such…I want you to know that I'm good. I had tests done when I last gave blood, and I haven't been with anyone since."

He swallowed the spontaneous question—*how long since someone else?*—and looked away. *Irrelevant. Too personal. None of your business.* And in his mind that justified not telling how long he'd been without. Instead he just nodded and said, "I'm clean."

There was an uncomfortable moment as their gazes connected and a measure of the unasked personal and intimate shivered between them. She made a rueful sound, half sigh, half laughter. "Okay, and now we're back at the awkward stage."

"Us, standing here wondering what to do next."

She smiled, appreciating his recall of their earlier conversation. "Except this time we're already in the bedroom."

"Naked."

"All over."

To illustrate her meaning Angie's gaze dipped, and the mood took on a new sultriness, as if a blanket of heat billowed high before descending to settle heavily over their bodies. One silken finger traced the length of his nakedness. Her breathing hitched. His, more so, as she cupped and stroked him more firmly.

Nope, he wouldn't be having any trouble functionally. Not if he made it inside her body before embarrassing himself. And if she kept touching him like that, and looking at him with her eyes kinda hazed and her lips softly parted, then that was quite on the cards.

"Enough," he bit out sharply. Then to take the edge off he tried a laugh, a laugh that came out all raw and strained. "It's been a while."

She let him go and for a long silent moment she watched him with unsettling intensity, as if she was delving inside and grabbing hold of his fears and laying them out for open examination. *Oh, no. No, no, no.* Reflexively he slammed down the shutters on the tiny window of vulnerability he'd unintentionally revealed.

No more private stuff, no expectations, no emotions.

Something of the unspoken must have shown on his face, because her expression slowly transformed from I-have-questions intensity to now-where-were-we? teasing. Settling back on her heels, she pointed at an erection that didn't need any pointing out. "I thought you told me not to expect too much."

Okay, so this was better. This he could play along with. Frowning, he pretended to inspect himself. "Too much?"

"Guess there's only one way to find out."

Despite the sexy banter, there were no smiles and her eyes flared with dark heat as their gazes connected. "I guess so."

Slowly she reached out and touched his forearm in a barely there caress, then her hand slid down to link fingers, and slowly, inexorably she tugged him down onto the bed.

They came together in an unchoreographed duel for position. It wasn't elegant, but it was so hot Tomas swore he heard the slow sizzle as their limbs parried for optimum sensual contact. One of his thighs settled between hers, and he couldn't stop himself pressing into her heat.

She responded with a deep hum of satisfaction.

For a second their gazes collided and he felt such a jolt—a left-right combination punch of need and fear and dread and desire—that he immediately ducked down to her mouth. They met with lips and tongues, with teeth and passion, and Tomas closed his eyes against the onslaught.

He closed his eyes and thought, *yes!* I can shut it all out. I can dive into the carnal delight of French kissing, I can shape my hands over these curves and immerse myself in the pleasure of all the scents and textures of a woman's body. I can absorb the throaty sounds of a woman's enjoyment and I can stand the roar of need in my ears.

I can handle the rush of lust because that's all it is. Only sex.

His hand shaped one breast, his thumb rasped across the nipple and she sucked a breath from his mouth, an act so intimate he felt its effect raw and deep in his gut. He jammed his eyes closed tighter and breathed more deeply, until the indelibly delicious scent of her skin filled his lungs and his veins.

"What the hell did you bathe in?" he breathed huskily near her ear.

"Cinnamon and honey-milk."

And he gave a half-grunt of laughter because that's what he'd been about to ask. Honey-milk. She tasted so sweet, her skin was so soft and pliant. Unthinking he opened his eyes and saw her roll her head back against the sheets, her dark curls a wild and wanton spread against the white.

"That's what the bottle said." She blinked slowly. "Do you want to taste me?"

"Later," he growled because even the thought of going down on her damn near brought him undone. He could feel a rawness gathering inside, a desperation he didn't want to contain.

Her mouth tilted into a sultry smile. "I can hardly wait."

"Right now," he said, repositioning himself to settle thickly between her thighs, "It's this way."

"Okay," she whispered on a broken murmur of breath.

Okay. That's all this would be, he told himself as he deliberately drew out that initial slide of entry. This would be okay. Not wonderful. Not wild and untamed. Not earth-shattering or mind-altering. Just okay. All he had to do was take it easy, maintain control, keep his focus on the wall or the pillows or on visualizing the twisted thread of his restraint. He wouldn't look into her eyes, he wouldn't indulge in sweet words or tender kisses, and he wouldn't think about the incredible moist pleasure of her body molding to accommodate his penetration.

Slowly. Take it slowly.

Sweat broke out along his back and on his forehead as he stopped himself giving in to what his body craved. To just plunge into her, hard, fast, wild. He sucked in air through his teeth, stared harder at the beige wall, and then he felt the tremulous touch of her hand on his face.

"If you're worrying about the 'too much' comment, then don't."

For a moment he forgot himself and looked down, right into her eyes. Not teasing like her husky-voiced comment, but serious, intent, burning. He drew back slightly and then let himself go in one long hard drive that took him all the way inside and he couldn't contain the long, deep sound of satisfaction that rose from his throat.

Sweet, oh God she was sweet.

Tomas couldn't stand it—not the enraptured look on her face or the softening of her lips or the do-that-again challenge in her eyes. He had to look away, refocus. To remind himself that *she* wasn't sweet. Sex was sweet. Being enclosed in that velvet female sheathing, the silky slide as he withdrew and drove back again, the hot friction of flesh against flesh, of male against female. This sex was so sweet because it had been so long and he'd almost forgotten the intensity of the pleasure. It was okay to enjoy it, to let himself go a little, to ease back so he could touch her breasts and flatten his hand against her belly and imagine that this was about making a child.

Only sex. And if it succeeded, never again.

Conversely his mind railed and bucked against that possibility. This was so good he wanted to do it again and again and again. Abruptly he pulled back, almost all the way out, then thrust himself in to the hilt. Too good to contemplate never doing again and that was all right, too, he justified, because tonight he could do it again and again. He could because it was necessary to make the child he needed.

It wasn't about this rapidly escalating rapture, not about the gut-wrenching explosion of pleasure when his hand slid lower and thumbed her slick plump heart until she came apart in a shuddering cry that kept on going and going as he changed angles and drove into her until his own climax roared through him like a cyclone, rough and whirling and eddying through his rigid frame with uncontrollable force.

He could justify that he couldn't disconnect immediately, not while his heart thundered and his blood roared and his mind clamored with the image of his seed spilling deeply into her fertile core.

For a minute his whole being succumbed to the intensity of that image and he slumped forward, his nose buried in that sweet hot spot where her neck joined with her shoulder. Their heartbeats raced one against the other and he knew he should move but he couldn't, not until she took a slow, shuddering breath that echoed right through him.

They were that close.

Too close, and when her mouth touched the side of his face with the kind of tender intimacy he'd vowed to avoid, he suddenly found his strength. He was on his feet and into the bathroom before her kiss had cooled on his cheek. Shower controls turned to maximum, he stepped under the torrent and let the cold water savage him for a count of ten. Then he spread his legs and planted his arms against the cold tiles and let the water pound out the torpor of sexual satiation.

Somewhere at the back of his mind he imagined it might also pound away a nagging sense of dissatisfaction. Not with the sex—jeez, but that had been unbelievably satisfying. No, it was something deeper, probably tied up with those earlier chills of fear, but even after ten minutes or so of water-torture he couldn't put a finger on the cause.

And he couldn't stand here any longer, not without turning blue. Adjusting the temperature mix, he rolled back his head and let the warmth hit him full in the face. Then he raked his wet hair back from his face, turned off the taps and reached for a towel.

Bare-assed, he padded back to the bedroom, his muscles tightening reflexively with every step. She'd turned the lights out, he realized, but enough light filtered in from the city outside for him to make out the figure curled up on the bed. Motionless. Asleep.

He exhaled a long, audible breath. No need for post-coital conversation or cuddling. She'd left plenty of the bed for him, enough of a buffer zone that he could crawl in under the covers and spread out in his usual fashion without any contact. That didn't help him relax. As the minutes passed he grew tenser, more wide-awake and so attuned to the silence that he swore he could hear each ticking minute on the noiseless bedside clock.

Possibly because he was concentrating so hard on anything besides the soft sound of Angie's breathing.

Damn her, how could she be so relaxed? Had what they'd done been so exhausting…or so meaningless that she could roll over and go to sleep within minutes? He turned restlessly and shucked off the eiderdown quilt. So, okay, he'd been gone more than a few minutes, but still….

Did she think that was it? One time lucky? And what about her earlier invitation. *Do you want to taste me?*

His body reacted instantly, extravagantly, as if she'd whispered the incendiary words into his ear right then. Turning impatiently on his side didn't help. Not when he could see the rise and fall of her breasts under the pure white sheet. *I can hardly wait,* she'd said.

Well, hell, he'd waited long enough. They only had this one night. What a waste to spend it watching her sleep when he was obviously up for making certain.

It was okay to smooth her hair away from her throat and taste her there, he figured. It was okay to kiss his way over her shoulder and whisper "wake up, Angie" when she stirred restlessly and rolled onto her side. Fine to kiss his way down the length of her naked spine and to learn the multitude of curves and valleys that made up her generous body. And when she stretched sleepily and pressed back into him with a lazy sigh, how could he not reach around to cup her breasts and rub her nipples and wake her by stroking her slick, wet heat?

When she rocked hard against him and murmured "already?" he took her like that, in a long, lazy joining, and again in the predawn quiet when the pace was slow and sensuous with enough time to recognize his earlier bout of fear for what it was.

Not performance anxiety or any sense of disloyalty to the wife he still loved, but fear that he would enjoy this—enjoy *her*—so much that he would never want it to end. That he'd want to twist his fingers into her chain and drag her mouth down to his, to swallow her cries of release whole and absorb them into his body.

That he would want this to go on and on and never end.

Angie woke to the glare of morning sun streaming through the window and the low sound of conversation. Frowning slightly, she pushed up on her elbows and strained her ears. Not the TV she realized, shoving her hair back from her face, but real voices in the adjoining room. Before she had a chance to identify words out of the indistinguishable drone, her attention diverted to the scent of food and her nose twitched and her stomach growled. Between no dinner and the…um…strenuous night, she was famished.

As she swung her legs out of bed she stretched her arms and back. And winced. Oh, yes, it had, indeed, been a most strenuous night. Satisfying in many ways, promising in many ways, even if she hated the many times he'd refused to meet her gaze, the times he'd chosen the darkness of closed eyes over the emotional connection of their joining.

Even if the notion that he'd needed to wash the scent of their lovemaking from his body still rubbed raw against her heart.

Slowly she started for the same bathroom. Vaguely she realized that the voices had stopped, and when she heard the thump of a door closing, she stopped dead. Surely he wouldn't just leave? Surely. But her heart shifted with uncomfortable doubt as she resumed her trip toward the bathroom. Just shy of the door, a sixth sense made her swing her gaze back…and there he was, standing in the doorway between bedroom and sitting-room, watching her.

He, she noticed immediately, was dressed. Unlike her. Ridiculous, after all they'd done in the night, to feel so exposed. He'd seen pretty much everything, from much closer than the width of a hotel bedroom.

"I ordered breakfast," he said evenly.

A good start, she thought. Excellent really, since she would have bet on much awkwardness this morning.

"I'm famished, but I just need a quick shower before I eat." She smiled broadly, in appreciation of him ordering breakfast, *and* still being here to share it. "Will you save me something?"

"I've already eaten. With Rafe."

Angie stiffened. That explained the other voice. Yet… "You invited your brother to breakfast?"

"He invited himself."

Aah, now *that* made more sense. And explained the closing door.

"Does he know…?" She gestured between them, indicating the meaning she couldn't put into words. *That I'm here, in your bedroom, naked?*

"No, and that's the way I'd prefer we kept it." He shifted his weight from one booted foot to the other. "Look, I just rang the airport. My pilot's ready to go. I have to get moving."

"Well, I'll have my shower and breakfast and go straight down to work, I expect." She managed a carefree shrug, but since she was standing naked in the full morning light, she couldn't quite bring herself to stroll over and casually kiss him goodbye. Which is the comeback she would have liked, to prove that though her heart had just taken a plummeting nosedive, she could handle this. He'd told her not to expect too much. She knew this would be a long haul, this getting past his hurt and distance to the man inside.

Last night she'd taken the first step, and that was only the start.

Despite his gotta-go message, he still hadn't moved from the doorway, however, and Angie discerned he had more to say. Ever helpful, she raised her eyebrows, inviting him to spit it out.

"Call me," he said, "as soon as you know something."

"You'll be the first to know."

He nodded stiffly.

And Angie couldn't help herself, the words just kind of bubbled out. "Do you think I will have to call? Do you think last night was a success?"

Which, in retrospect, was a ridiculous thing to ask. She'd read the literature. Even at the right time of month, with all the planets in alignment and karma beaming down from the stars, a certain percentage of women didn't conceive. It wasn't as if she'd ever tried before. She didn't know, for sure, that she was the perfect candidate she'd promoted herself as the night before.

And her ridiculous questions had obviously made Tomas as uncomfortable as a ringer with a burr in his swag, because now he couldn't meet her eyes. He stared toward the window and beyond, his expression so tricky and unreadable that she longed to climb inside his head.

"If you are—" his gaze shifted back to her face "—will you want to keep working?"

"I told you. My job here is temporary."

"You know Rafe will give you another job at the drop of a hat. Alex, too."

"And what about you? Do you have a job for me on Kameruka Downs?"

His eyes narrowed. "You're joking."

"Why would you think that?"

"Because I wouldn't—" He stopped abruptly, lips a tight line.

"Because you don't want me around?"

"Because there's no job for you there."

The pain she felt was, no doubt, her heart bottoming out of that slow-fall plummet with a sickening crash. "I'll let you know the result, once I know," she said, painfully aware that she was still standing here, having this momentous conversation, stark naked.

Tomas started to turn, paused. "Angie…thank you."

For being such a sport? For not pushing the job issue? For not making this morning-after a train wreck?

It was her turn to nod tightly. "You're welcome."

And then he was gone, probably bolting as fast as his boots would take him, to the airport and the company plane that would transport him back to his territory.

Kameruka Downs, where she was no longer welcome.

Seven

For two weeks Angie hummed through life in a cheerful glow of hopefulness. When she closed the door on that hotel suite—after an indulgently long shower and an extravagantly big breakfast—she closed the door on all doubts and despondency. She left them there in the dark, shut away from the shining light of her optimism.

Only sex? Bull! She'd felt the connection, the specialness, the rightness of their lovemaking.

As for Tomas…well, she could make allowances. He'd been even more nervous than Angie, and he didn't have the crutch of a lifetime of fantasies for support. She'd seriously unsettled him with that revelation, and she'd unnerved him more with the emotion she couldn't completely contain when they'd finally come together.

Plus, in his own words, it had been a while.

Her mind had drifted back to that comment with vexing regularity. A while, as in, not since Brooke? Could he have been celibate that long?

Knowing Tomas…yes. Because that's how he would honor his vows, yet that thought caused a churning storm of conflict in Angie. The very qualities that drew her to this man—his steadfastness, his loyalty, his constancy and conviction—could also be the downfall of any hope of a future with him.

He loved Brooke. He probably believed he would never love again. Yet Angie knew deep in her heart that she was his woman, and she used that confidence to staunch the rebellious doubts as she worked through two weeks without any calls from or contact with Kameruka Downs. He was busy, she reminded herself. This was his busiest time of year with the cattle business. Besides, *she* was to call *him,* she reassured herself, whenever her hungry gaze drifted to the phone late at night.

Then her hand would cradle her belly and her heart would skitter with a mix of nerves and excitement as she contemplated the prospect of Tomas's baby growing there. And she would fall asleep with a smile on her lips and optimism warm in her heart.

This morning, when she visited the bathroom, fate and the female cycle rudely snuffed out that light.

Naturally it was Monday and she couldn't slink back to bed. Predictably it was a stinking grey Monday, the kind that decides to dump its wet load of misery on a woman's shoulders when she's running to catch the bus. And because she was in no mood for company, Rafe came to wander aimlessly around her workspace as soon as he arrived at the office.

That happened to be about five minutes after she'd tossed her rose-colored glasses in the bin beside her desk, along with the pregnancy-test kit she'd bought ahead of time and stored in the back of her filing cabinet. She knew the second Rafe's miss-nothing eyes settled on the discarded box.

Why had she given in to that silly fit of hormonal pique? Why hadn't she just left the kit where it was? She hadn't needed to trash the damn thing!

A small frown lined her boss's forehead. "Is that what I think it is?"

"That's none of your business."

His gaze lifted at her sharp tone. "It appears to be unopened."

"How observant." It was hard not to sound snarky when Rafe—dammit—was pushing aside papers to perch on the edge of her desk.

"Do I take it this is bad news?"

She clicked her mouse and stared hard at the computer screen.

"Because I always thought it was bad news when the lines turned pink."

Eyes narrowed in irritation, she swung back to face him. "In your situation, that would be good news…or have you forgotten the baby you're supposed—"

"So, you did do it."

"What?"

"You and Tomas. That night in the suite. I wondered."

Yet he hadn't said a word. *She* wondered—

"I didn't say anything in case nothing came of it," he said, finishing her thought. He glanced back at her bin. "Is that what the unopened test means?"

"I'm not pregnant, if that's what you're asking."

And because she couldn't stand the sharp perceptiveness of his gaze—or the flicker of sympathy in his eyes—

she turned back to her computer. Tapped at a couple of keys before she realized she hadn't opened a document. The computer beeped back at her, something that sounded like *you dolt.* And she was the stupid, idiotic queen of dolts for imagining she could do this, for thinking that one night would instantly provide a baby, and for wanting it so much. Dammit, and now she had to put up with her boss sitting there looking at her with pity and—

"What are you going to do about it?" he asked, and she whirled on him in a flash of fury.

"What are *you* doing about it? You, also being part of this pact. Why should it be up to me? And how about Alex—has he set a date yet?"

"Last I heard, he and Susannah are still in negotiation."

Which meant no date, no marriage, no baby, since Alex had decided that marriage had to come first. "And you?"

"I'm still considering my options."

"Too much choice?"

Instead of grinning or winking or chipping in with the usual Rafe-line, he looked at her steadily. "Or maybe I can't find the right woman to make a baby with."

The right woman, the right mother, the perfect candidate. Angie's heartbeat sounded thick and loud in the sudden quiet. "Do you think Tomas found the right woman?"

"Do you?"

Yeesh, but she hated questions tossed back in her face. Twelve hours ago she knew the answer, unequivocally, but now? Had so much changed? Or was this only a wet-day hormone funk? She stared at the blankness of her computer screen a moment, and the only answer she found was the truth. "I want to make more than a baby with him. I want to make him live and laugh and love again."

Rafe grinned. And winked. "Attagirl."

Angie scowled back at him, but somewhere inside she felt the tiny flicker of hope. "Fat lot of good it will do me."

"My brother needs someone like you. Someone with the balls—"

"Thank you very much!"

"—to keep pushing and prodding so he doesn't hole up in his shell like a hermit crab. He needs someone who loves him enough to not give up."

"You think?"

"He needs you more than he needs this baby, Ange."

Holy Henry, she hoped so. Yet, if Rafe believed it—if he could sit there and recite with such conviction the belief engraved deep in her heart… "Do you suppose your father thought the same thing?" she asked slowly. "That he was using the will clause to push Tomas to find someone else?"

"Maybe." In silence, they both considered this a minute. Then Rafe shook his head. "Nah, there's too many things that could have gone wrong, the way he worded the clause."

"I guess."

"What matters is making sure everything goes right from here on in. You need to be in his face, Ange, showing him what he's missing."

"What do you suggest? That I turn up on his doorstep and chirp, 'Honey, I'm home'?"

Rafe grinned. "You're reading my mind."

It took Angie a moment to realize he wasn't joking. She wet her lips nervously. "What, exactly, are you thinking?"

"Two weeks, right? Until you can next make babies?"

Angie nodded.

"What if I fly you out there a bit earlier…?" Not really a question, since he didn't wait for an answer. He picked up her desk calendar and studied it. When he looked up his eyes held a wicked glitter. "You know what this Saturday is?"

"Um…the twentieth?"

"The Ruby Creek Races."

Angie frowned. The Ruby Creek weekend was an outback institution, more about socializing than horse-racing, but what did it have to do with her situation? "You want to go? You think I should go? Do you think Tomas will be going?"

"Unlikely. He doesn't get out much these days. No, what I'm thinking is all the staff will be going and he'll be home alone."

Until she arrived. Angie's pulse fluttered. "He won't like it."

"Does that matter?"

She smiled slowly and the glow of hope spread strong and rosy through her whole body. "No. I don't suppose that it does."

Tomas recognized the sound of the Carlisle Company plane coming in low over the Barakoolie ridge without lifting his gaze from the weaners he was tailing. He figured it was Alex or Rafe dropping in to visit with their mother. A wasted trip, since Maura had flown down to another of their stations to supervise the muster after the manager broke his leg. Tomas would have gone himself except…

His chest tightened as he recalled the plea in his mother's pained eyes—a look that had cow-kicked him right where he lived. He knew what she couldn't say. *I'm lost and I'm hurting. I need to be busy, occupied, working as hard as my body can take. It's the only way to live through this grief.*

Oh, yeah, he knew better than anyone the benefits of physical exhaustion. Not a cure, but a salve to deaden the acute pain and a bandage dressing for the soul-deep loneliness. A means to fill the days and a way to find the salvation of sleep in a marriage bed suddenly left half-empty. So, yeah, he'd let Mau go with his blessing, and if either of his brothers gave him grief over it… After several weeks of fourteen- and fifteen-hour days he felt brutal enough to knock them both on their Armani-clad asses.

Thinking about that outcome gave him a grim satisfaction as he watched the King Air bank and turn before coming in low on its final approach to the airstrip. The young colt he was training jigged and danced beneath him. And if his pulse skipped in time with his fractious mount, that wasn't because some rogue part of him remembered the last time one of company planes had sat on the Kameruka airstrip.

The way she'd tried to kiss him. The day she'd sowed the idea of only-sex in his brain.

"Easy boy," he soothed. "It's just a big old noisy bird." *With a big old noisy pilot.*

He identified Rafe as the pilot by the way he approached his landing. Not sure and steady like Alex, but in a flamboyant rush.

The colt tossed his head, and with knees and thighs Tomas directed his attention back to the cattle. "We have a job to do, Ace," he murmured. "Keep your eye on the prize."

He didn't turn back toward the strip. He would see his brother soon enough, whether he wanted to or not. And even though this was officially a holiday weekend on Kameruka, with all his staff away at the races or visiting friends or simply sitting it out at the local bar, his time off was this: training a young colt to tail cattle. Later he'd fly a bore check in the station Cessna. And there was a gate hinge to weld on the Boolah round-yard. All the stock horses and dogs to be fed.

Only when he was good and ready, would he return home to his visitor.

* * *

The sun had started its descent behind the rugged western cliffs of Killarney Gorge before Tomas returned to the homestead. His narrowed gaze scanned the deepening shadows of the veranda and, sure enough, found Rafe. He didn't care. He was resigned to enduring his brother's smart-ass company this evening. In fact, he was looking forward to crossing words if not swords—either would suit his mood. But first, he was looking forward to a long cold beer and a longer hot shower.

"Rafe," he said in greeting, as he hit the veranda and kept moving.

"Pleased to see you, too. I was getting bored with my own company."

"No kidding." He paused with the door half-open. "I'd have saved you the tedium if you'd rung first."

"You'd have laid on hot and cold running housemaids?"

"I'd have told you Ruby Creek was on."

Rafe chuckled softly. "I knew that. I'm heading out there in the morning, but I thought I'd spend the night with Mau first. I'm surprised she's not home yet."

"She's over at Killarney, mustering."

"Better that she's keeping busy." No surprise, no censure, barely a pause to digest the news. "I'll fly down tomorrow and see her."

"Only if you've got a couple of days free. She'll be out in the back country by now." And they both knew that no one—not even Rafe—could land a twin-engine there.

"How's she doing?"

Tomas let the door swing shut and tipped his hat back. "She's coping."

For a quiet minute they were in accord, everything else forgotten in shared concern for their mother. Worry that she may sink back into the same depression as after she lost her baby daughter—their sister—so many years ago. Rafe made a scoffing noise and shook his head. "Why didn't he just leave her one of the stations to run? That would have made more sense than this grandchild thing."

"Is that why you think he did it? For Mau?"

"Don't you?"

Tomas let his breath go in a long sigh. "Yup, I do."

"Do you reckon it'll make any difference? That she'll buy we're doing this because we want to?"

"Does it matter in the end? If she gets the grandchild to dote on?"

"Point." Rafe expelled a long, audible breath. "I'll fly out next weekend to see her."

Tomas nodded, but he could see there was more going on in Rafe's head than the fact he'd wasted a trip. He looked almost…pained.

"What are you doing about the baby?" Tomas asked, taking a stab at what bothered his brother's usual carefree attitude. "Have you decided on a mother yet?"

"There's someone I'm hoping to bump into at Ruby Creek tomorrow."

Hence the look of a man headed for the gallows. If he didn't feel a barrowload of empathy, Tomas would have found his brother's situation funny—the last of the great playboys forced to choose one woman. He didn't ask for the lucky lady's name because the look on his brother's face reminded him of his own circumstances. Of Angie, who Rafe would have seen as recently as yesterday. It had been over two weeks. She'd said she'd call as soon as she knew. She should have called.

He scowled down at his boots, tried to find the words he needed down there. *How's Angie? Two simple words, one question. How hard was that?* Instead he found himself asking, "How's the hotel business?"

"Booming." Rafe stared at him a moment. "Can't say you've ever expressed an interest before. Is there a reason? Anything specific you wanted to know?"

Tomas gritted his teeth. Okay, all he had to do was ask. He took off his hat, slapped it against his thigh. "How's Angie?"

"Why don't you ask her yourself?"

Call her? His gut clenched and fisted. "Yeah, I guess I could phone her."

"I meant you should ask her. In person."

Tomas frowned. "In Sydney?"

"Inside." Rafe hitched a shoulder in that direction. "I think she mentioned something about taking a bath. She liked the look of that new spa you put in."

In *his* bathroom? Like hell!

Tomas barreled down the long hallway and shouldered through the half-open door. Yes, she'd taken a bath. In his bathroom. Wisps of steam wafted toward the open louver windows, and the moist sweet fragrance of honeyed bath oil still hung in the air.

The house had a half-dozen bathrooms and she'd had to use his? Dammit to hell and back…

He slapped his hand against the doorjamb, whipped around and his eyes narrowed in cold fury. His bedroom door lay open. Oh, no. No, no, no. *No.* A dozen long strides and he came to a grinding halt, everything locked up by the sight that greeted him through that open doorway.

Angie was bent over his bed, ratting through an open suitcase. Not that he took much notice of the suitcase, since she wore nothing but a towel. For a long minute his anger dissipated, swamped by the heated rush of a body remembering. The soft pliancy of her thighs. The full curves of her buttocks. The sheer carnal pleasure of sliding inside.

She stilled suddenly and turned, as if she'd heard the groan of his lust or the snarl of his restraint, and her eyes widened in surprise. Vaguely he was aware of something—hell, it could have been the crown jewels for all he noticed—drop from her fingers as she straightened.

"Hi."

The husky note of her greeting stroked his aroused glands like a velvet fist, and in that spun-out moment she had only to smile and unwrap her towel and he'd have forgotten every grievance. But she didn't smile. And she clutched the front of the towel with an edginess that reminded him of everything wrong with this picture.

Her body, in his towel, in his bedroom. Uninvited.

"What are you doing here?" he growled, low and mean.

"Looking for clothes. I was about to get dressed." Gathering her usual assurance, she let go the towel and leaned back into her luggage. "If I can just find my—"

"Dammit, Angie, you know that's not what I asked!"

She knew it and she had to know how much was revealed when she leaned over like that, but it didn't stop her dragging out the moment. Deliberately? Was she trying to provoke him? Entice him? Seduce him?

Tomas ground his teeth and forced his attention to her busy hands. They rummaged some more then paused, holding up a piece of ivory satin underwear that dangled from her fingertips like some blatant stroke-me invitation. Oh, yeah, this was deliberate, unsubtle and doomed for failure.

"Forget getting dressed," he barked. "We need to talk."

Her gaze skittered with the same edginess she'd displayed earlier. Good. This was his home, his territory, and he was calling the shots. She had cause to look nervous.

"Why didn't you call?"

"That's why I'm here," she said quietly. And as if her legs lost strength, she kind of flopped down onto the edge of his bed. "Instead of calling."

"You're pregnant?"

The thick ponytail on top of her head wobbled as she shook her head. "No. I'm not."

"Are you sure?"

"Pretty much."

"What does that mean? Did you do a test or not?"

Her backbone stiffened at his harsh tone, and her gaze snapped to his. "I mean," she said clearly, evenly, "that unless I'm one of those women who bleed even when they're pregnant, then I'm not."

Tomas let go an audible breath. Restless, unable to meet the steady darkness of her gaze and unsure how to respond, he paced to the window. Hesitated a second before turning around. "You okay with that?"

"I'm disappointed. What about you?"

How did he feel? Thrown. Rattled. Disgruntled. And, yeah, disappointed that she hadn't let him know. That she'd probably confided in Rafe first—why else would he have brought her out here?

"How long have you known?" he asked tightly.

"Only a day or two."

"You said your cycle was regular as clockwork. I can do the sums, Angie. Either you—"

"Okay." She jumped to her feet in a rush of fluttering towel and creamy skin. "I knew on Monday. Yes, I should have called, but I wanted to surprise you."

What? He scarcely believed his ears. This was supposed

to be a pleasant surprise? *Here I am, in your bedroom, aren't you glad?*

She sucked in a breath, as if preparing to say more, but the action caused the towel-tuck over her breasts to come right undone. Before she could regather the gaping sides, Tomas caught an eyeful of dark nipples and curved belly and feminine curls. His body blistered with instant heat, his groin tightened with instant desire, but he rejected the quickening of lust and fixed her with a hard, cold stare.

"I don't like surprises."

He walked to the dresser and stared for a full twenty seconds before he realized what was wrong. Her hairbrush, a tub of face cream, her neck-chain, were scattered carelessly amidst his neatly arrayed belongings.

Tomas's jaw set so hard he heard his teeth grind.

He didn't want this. He didn't want her here, not in his home, not in his bedroom, not in his days and his nights.

With one fisted hand he scooped up her things and tossed them into her suitcase. In another second he'd gathered up all the gauzy bras and filmy panties that had spilled onto his bed, and jammed the lid shut on it all.

He was fuming that she'd pulled this surprise-him stunt, that she'd thought she could take over his bedroom, that she'd brought all that skimpy underwear with her…for what? They were having sex, not a seduction. He clicked the snaps shut on her case and his icy rage turned to steam.

"I hope you didn't buy all that specially," he said, straightening with the luggage in his hand.

In silence she'd watched him, not objecting, not commenting, although her eyes now flashed with indignation. "You don't like nice lingerie?"

"It's a waste of money if you bought it for me."

"Actually, I bought it for myself. I never thought for a

minute that you'd wear a G-string." She smiled silkily. "Although I do like how satin feels against my skin. Maybe you should feel it sometime."

Tomas refused to let her taunt affect him, refused to picture her wearing a satin G-string and nothing else, refused to imagine his hands skimming over her curves, touching, feeling, caressing. Narrow-eyed he glared back at her. "It looks like I'll have to."

"Are you saying you want to try again?"

"I take it that's why you're here."

"Yes," she answered calmly. "Bad news, I'm not pregnant. Good news, we get to do it all over again. If that's what you want."

Eight

Oh, yeah, he wanted, but this time he was setting the rules—starting with not in his bed. Suitcase in hand, he turned toward the door. "You'll have your own bedroom. That's not negotiable, Angie."

"If you want me out of your bedroom—" her eyes flashed a challenge "—you'll have to carry me."

He only hesitated long enough to think: *dentist, throbbing tooth, get it over with quick.* Eyes fixed on hers, he marched across the room, picked her up like a sack of chaff and tossed her over his shoulder.

She wiggled, she kicked, she punched. Against his shoulder he could feel the soft schmoosh of her breasts but he kept on walking. The towel rode up and his hand ended up cupping her bare backside, but he gritted his teeth and didn't stop until he'd dumped her inside the best of the guest bedrooms. Too bad if Rafe was using it, he was too damn mad to care. "This is your room and when we do it, we do it here. When are you fertile?"

"You did the sums before."

So he did them again, counting off the days on his fingers. "Next weekend."

"How many times?"

He'd turned to leave, had actually taken his first step out into the corridor, but her question stilled him. He could feel her eyes boring into the back of his neck, could feel their dark heat and fierce indignation.

"How many times are we doing it?" she asked again. "The book I read says a woman can conceive if she has intercourse any time up to five days before ovulation and twenty-four hours afterward. Conception isn't an exact science."

"I'm well aware of that." He turned and pinned her in place with an uncompromising look. "The article I read stated the optimum time as two days before and the day of ovulation. And you told me you're a twenty-eight-day clock."

"You're choosing three days of unregulated, unprotected, whenever-you-feel-like-it, however-you-want-it sex over six? Yeesh, Tomas, you're the only man I know who'd prefer that option!"

"Not whenever, however. Once a night, missionary position, in your bed." The exasperated sound she choked out turned his voice even colder while heat of every hue pumped through his blood. "This isn't personal preference. This is to preserve sperm count and let gravity do its bit."

"That's such an old wives' tale!"

"I have a housekeeper," he continued coldly, ignoring her interjection, "and a mother who visits regularly. I don't want either to know about this unless there's a positive result to tell. Either way, they'll both be here long after you've gone."

The expression in her eyes turned from willful to stunned in one blink of her long, dark lashes. Yeah, what he'd said was harsh but he wouldn't back down. If you gave Angie an inch, she always took a hundred miles. If he gave her access to his bed, she would keep on chipping away, wanting more and more of a life he had no intention of sharing, with her or anyone.

He watched her nostrils flare as she sucked in a breath, saw a grim determination replace the hurt in her eyes. "So, if this is going to be all clandestine, how will I know when to lie on my back and expect you?"

Tomas clenched his jaw. "You'll know."

"How is that?" she cocked her head on the side, all fake sweet-voiced curiosity. "Will there be some secret code?"

"You'll know when I turn up in your bed."

Angie hated everything about that hurtful snarky exchange, but she did accept his edict on separate bedrooms. It was his home, after all, and she had arrived uninvited. In retrospect, that hadn't been such a great idea. And if she thought he'd been hostile with her…

Five days later her body still did a kind of internal shudder and wince remembering the unpleasantness of their dinner with Rafe that night.

All her fault.

She should have called and let Tomas know she wasn't pregnant. She should have allowed him—not his brother—a say in what transpired next. Backing a stubborn man into the proverbial corner was not the way to win his cooperation. Lord knows, she came from a household steeped in testosterone. She should have known better.

She should have left his bedroom with better grace and some dignity, too. She shouldn't have let him light a match to her temper. And she definitely should not have kept pushing and provoking until he ground out that line about after-she'd-gone. Mostly she wasn't one to dwell on should-haves and most of that list she'd put well behind her by Thursday—all except the leaving thing and that bothered her deeply.

If he wouldn't let her stay, then how could she prove herself and her love? If he was never home and their paths crossed as rarely as they'd done in the past five days, then how could he see that she'd fitted happily back into station life?

She didn't assume he was avoiding her. It was a hectic time with mustering and branding and weaning and trucking out stock for sale and fattening. Tomas was responsible for managing a hundred thousand head of cattle and fifty employees. He was a busy man. So busy that he'd neglected to tell her he was flying out on a three-day visit to the company's eastern feed-lots.

She simmered and seethed inside for a good twenty-four hours, but what could she do? She could prepare for his return, that's what. She could make sure he *did* notice her seamless integration into his home and station life, and she could do so without another sharp-worded confrontation.

A few casual questions to a head stockman and she had an estimated time for the boss's return. She prepared dinner herself and chose the perfect wine accompaniment from Chas's extensive cellar. She soaked for a good hour in the honey and cinnamon bath-milk she'd bought especially for the trip—the same one she'd used in the hotel that night. "For you, Tomas," she stated with some defiance as she poured a liberal dose into the tub. "Same as all the pretty underwear."

Oh, and she gave the housekeeping staff the night off.

Tonight was the first of her three nights with Tomas, and she intended on making the most of it.

Despite the good food, the wine and the satin she'd chosen to wear next to her bath-softened skin, Angie didn't go for a full-out seduction scene. In the interests of subtlety—and not scaring him off—she scuttled the candles and flowers, and left the stereo turned off. That would help, too, with hearing his incoming plane.

Ready early, she couldn't stand still. She fussed over the lasagna and greens and bread rolls she'd baked earlier. She applied a third coat of Nude Shimmy polish and wandered restlessly around the gardens while her nails dried and the sun clocked off for the day. She even considered straightening her hair, just to fill some time.

But when she looked into the mirror at the mass of curls, she remembered Tomas saying he didn't like sleek. She set down the straightening tool and smiled slowly. "Oh, yeah. I rather like it wild, too."

Except she wasn't thinking about her hair.

She huffed out a breath, hot with memories and keen with anticipation, and eyed her reflection in the mirror. She looked like a woman thinking about sex. Heat traced the line of her cheekbones and glowed dark in her eyes. And when she stood up and braced her shoulders, she felt the sweet tug of arousal in her breasts and satin panties.

Perhaps she should really surprise him and take them off. Perhaps she would after she'd fortified her bravery with a glass of merlot.

Yes, she needed a glass of wine. And to check the meal one more time. She straightened the neckline of her white gypsy top, smoothed the sitting-down wrinkles from her jeans, and set off for the kitchen at the opposite end of the house. With every step she could feel the friction of her clothes against each sensitive peak and fold of her body. Perhaps she should take everything off and *really* surprise him…although that would take a lot more than one glass of bravado!

Smiling at herself, she pushed through the kitchen door and came to a stunned standstill.

Tomas was home.

Right there in the middle of the kitchen, actually, although he hadn't yet noticed her arrival. He stood in profile, a tall, dark, dusty hunk with a long-neck bottle in his hand. She watched his head tilt back as he raised the beer to his lips. Watched the movement of his throat as he drank…and she drank in his almost sybaritic enjoyment of that first long, slow pull from the cold bottle.

In that moment he wasn't Tomas Carlisle, heir apparent to Australia's richest cattle empire. He wasn't any "Prince of the Outback." He was just an ordinary cowboy at the end of a hellishly long working day.

A quiver of pure desire slid through her body, from the tingling in her scalp all the way to the freshly painted tips of her toes. She wanted to walk right up and kiss him on his drink-cooled lips and breathe the commingled scents of horse and leather and Kameruka dust on his skin. But more even than the physical, she longed to share dinner without sniping and harsh words. She wanted to let the evening flow naturally all the way to the moment when they stood in unison and walked hand in hand to bed.

Was that too much to ask?

Suddenly the hand holding the bottle stilled halfway back down from his mouth, and Angie had enough time to answer her own question—*yes, definitely too much*—before his head turned slowly her way. She could feel the tension in her bones and knew it seeped into the innocent kitchen air. And all she could think to say was, "You're home."

He grunted—possibly an acknowledgment, possibly a commentary on the intelligence of her opening remark.

"I didn't hear your plane," she continued, with a sweeping gesture toward the roof.

"I'm not surprised."

Angie frowned. She'd turned off the music so she wouldn't miss his arrival. "What do you mean?"

"You were in the bath."

What? That was hours ago. And how did he know she—

"You wouldn't have heard me above the music."

Holy Henry, he must have been in the house earlier. How could she not have known? Angie blanched, remembering how she'd belted out whatever lyrics she knew and improvised the rest. "Why didn't you say something?" she asked on a note of dismay.

"I only came in to change."

And since he wasn't laughing or looking horrified, perhaps he hadn't heard her singing. Relaxing a smidge, she now realized the significance of her first impression. He wasn't dressed for a business trip but for get-down-and-dirty cattle work, because he'd returned early and come to the house to change. Her gaze slid over his dusty blue Western shirt and lingered on the Wranglers he wore so well.

"What's going on, Angie?" he asked with a hint of suspicion. And when her gaze flew back to his face she caught him giving her a similar once-over. "Where is everyone?"

"I gave Manny—" who'd been rostered for kitchen duty "—the night off."

"Why?"

"I thought it would be easier, given you want to keep this just between us."

He'd started to lift his beer again, but hesitated as the knowledge of what that meant arced between them, hot and sultry and heavy as a summer's night. At least that's how Angie's body felt. Without breaking eye contact he took another long drink, another long swallow. "Is that why you're all dressed up?"

She almost laughed out loud, remembering how many times she'd changed her clothes in an attempt to dress *down.* But, still, she liked that he knew she'd made an effort. She wasn't afraid of letting him know she wanted him.

Slowly she crossed the kitchen floor, closing down the space between them, never losing that hot eye-to-eye connection. She ached to kiss him, to hold him, to have him right here and now. But beyond the surface of his blue-heat eyes she detected a flicker of wariness that held her back. Instead of reaching for the man, she reached for his beer and lifted it to her lips.

As she drank she watched *him* swallow, and desire beat so hard in her veins she swore she could feel its echo in every cell of her body.

"You're why I gave Manny the night off and you're why I'm wearing satin underwear," she said huskily. "But first you're having a shower, and then we're having dinner. I don't know about you, but I'm starving."

While he showered Tomas tried to work up a decent sense of outrage. Without asking she'd used his bathroom again. She'd given *his* staff the night off. He'd let her know, in plain language, how this would happen and she'd gone ahead and set up a seduction scene.

But it was hard to maintain rage in a body tight and hot

with anticipation. *She's waiting out there alone,* it throbbed, *for you. She's wearing satin underwear,* it pulsed, *for you. She's starving,* it thundered, *for you.*

Despite the insistent ache of arousal he forced himself to dress unhurriedly, to arrive slowly, to sit and eat and talk. The wine helped. After one glass he realized he wasn't going to ignite every time their eyes met in an awkward conversational lapse, or each time his gaze was drawn to the erotic caress of her thumb over the rim of her wineglass.

It only felt that way.

He shifted in his chair, surreptitiously rearranging that insistent ache of arousal. He was a sad case. There she was, chatting away about the innocuous and everyday, oblivious to the effect of her unconscious glassware fondling. Lucky he'd worn roomy chinos because sitting down in jeans, in his condition, would have been murder.

"Hello?"

He looked up to find her waving her hands to attract his attention.

"You didn't hear a word of that, did you?"

"I was—" Tomas frowned "—thinking."

"Looks serious."

Yeah, deadly.

She eyed him a second. "About the trip you made to Queensland? Is there a problem?"

His pulse kicked up a notch as he met her eyes across the table and imagined telling her his real problem. *I've been at least half-hard ever since I hauled your naked backside into your bedroom five nights ago. The waiting's killing me, Angie. Let's skip the pretense and—*

"Because I'm all ears. If you need to talk it through."

Abruptly she put down her cutlery and pushed her plate away, and the decisiveness of her action startled the hormone haze from his mind. She thought he was distracted by cattle problems. He was dying for action, and she wanted to talk.

Shaking his head in disbelief, he pushed his plate away, too. "There's no problem with the business."

"Good." She smiled, and damn her, started to play with her glass again. "Yesterday I read that feature article in *The Cattleman,* about how you're now considered the innovator, the market leader. It seems you've made a lot of changes since you took over managing the northern stations."

"Necessary changes."

"And production has increased fifteen percent."

"We've had some good seasons."

"And good management."

Half distracted by the play of her pale-tipped fingers on her wineglass, he didn't answer. Idly he wondered where she was going with this, but mostly he didn't feel any need to answer. She was right. Good management had increased Carlisle's productivity.

"Can I ask you something…about the will clause?"

The idle part of his brain clicked to full alert, driving the lingering heat of arousal from his synapses. Not because of the question, but the hint of non-Angie guardedness in her delivery. Tension straightened his spine as he made a go-ahead gesture.

"Here's the way I understand it—correct me if I'm wrong. If you fail to produce this baby between the three of you, you won't inherit ownership of Kameruka Downs or any of the other cattle stations. The company would keep ownership and the board overall control?"

Tomas nodded. Correct so far.

"So, I can't see the board replacing you as manager or

kicking you out of your home, not when you're making the company money hand over fist."

"It's not the same as ownership. That's what I've worked toward, always." He met her eyes across the table. "More than ever the past couple of years."

"Because of Brooke?"

Yes, because he no longer had Brooke. What else did he have to work toward, to strive for, if not this place?

"Do you want to talk about it?" she asked, and the husky catch to her voice brought his gaze rocketing back to hers. To the undisguised light of emotion in her eyes. "Do you want to talk about—"

"No, I don't," he said curtly.

"Fair enough. That's your prerogative. But any time you change your mind…"

He didn't bother responding. He didn't want to talk about Brooke and he didn't want to debate why. And he sure as hell didn't need her watching him with those serious, solemn eyes that made him want to run a mile…and made him want to lash out at everything wrong about what happened with Brooke. Everything he wouldn't let happen again.

The silence stretched between them another tense minute before he saw her start to stack their plates and set them aside. Her hands with their pale glossy nails spread on the table, providing leverage as she stood. And he looked up to find her watching him, those serious, solemn eyes filled with all kinds of promises of temptation and salvation as she extended her hand toward him.

"Let's go to bed."

Five minutes ago he would have taken that hand and invitation and they probably wouldn't have made it to any bedroom. But now… No, he couldn't touch her. Not in this mood, not with so much emotion and despair and desperate need roiling in his gut.

He couldn't need her like that—he wouldn't allow himself.

"I have to work on the books," he said.

"Okay. I'll pack the dishwasher then I'll come help you."

"No, Angie. You can't help me."

She'd started to gather up the dishes, but paused, her eyes rising slowly to lock on his. "I thought I already was."

"In one way. That's all."

The message hummed between them and for several taut, electric seconds he didn't know that she would accept it. "I don't want to fight about this," he said softly. "I don't want to fight with you, Angie."

"Oh, me, either," she said in a breathy rush. "Those things we said to each other the night I got here—I don't want it to be like that between us. Let me help you, Tomas."

He set his jaw, his resolve, the steel in his heart and his eyes. "Don't ask for what I can't give."

Emotion shimmered in the fathomless depths of her eyes, but she nodded and mouthed one word. Okay. With careful hands she gathered up the pile of dishes, and as she walked from the room he heard one tiny clatter of crockery, as if her hands trembled and then regrouped. At the door, she hesitated and turned. "Will I see you later?"

Tomas nodded. Later when this maelstrom of emotions stopped whipping through his body, when he'd controlled the persistent pounding need to stop her leaving and yell, yes, I want to talk. I want to talk if it eases the pain and the guilt and this bitter knowledge that I could have done better. That I failed my wife.

"Later," he said hoarsely. "Yes."

Nine

Two hours, Tomas told himself, and to prove he was in control of mind and body and emotions he stretched it to two hours twenty. Then he came to her room and quietly closed the door behind him. Head raised and nostrils flared, he waited for his eyes to adjust to the midnight dark.

It wasn't like night in the city. This was outback dark, an intense blackness that amplified the other senses to an acute pitch. He could smell the warm female scent of her body. Could hear the quick in-out whisper of her breathing.

Was she awake? Lying in the dark waiting? Craving the intense pleasure of that first skin to skin contact?

He shed his clothes quickly, felt the night air stroke him like a lover's warm sigh. His skin was as hot and tight as a steer hide stretched to dry in the summer sun. As he stripped off his underwear the fleeting brush of his hand caused his erection to jerk with need.

He sucked in a tense breath, half afraid of the edginess to this lust. Half afraid that the edges were keened with loneliness and need and yearning for more than hot bodies meeting in the darkness. The distant call of a night bird echoed in the dark, a high haunting two-note summons to its mate. Closer he heard the soft stirring of sheets, and his sex quickened in instant response. Its call to mate.

He started toward the bed, and despite the darkness he could make out the slow stretch of her arms above her head. As he stopped by the bed she made a throaty sound of welcome. "You're here."

"I thought you'd be asleep."

She shifted again, rolling onto her side and pushing aside the bedclothes. "I was waiting for you."

He sat on the edge of the mattress and her hand glided over his back, a whisper of sensation that reverberated through his body and pulsed in his blood and his sex. So did her scent—the familiar sweet fragrance of skin steeped in honey and cinnamon milk. The same as the day she'd arrived. The same as in Sydney when he'd yearned to taste her.

Tonight he would.

Then it wouldn't matter if he lasted or not, if first he gave her pleasure.

"Was there really paperwork?" she asked as he settled beside her.

He didn't answer, except to groan a deep thankful note as her arms and her legs wrapped around to draw him flush with her body. He didn't answer because he forgot the question when she rocked against him, breast to chest, groin to groin, soft to hard. Unerringly he found her lips in the dark and kissed her deeply, a long, wet play of tongues and mouths and throaty murmurings that seemed to hang suspended in the heavy curtain of night. He didn't close his eyes. He didn't have to hide in the darkness, didn't have to fear what he might see in her eyes or what she might learn from his.

Slowly he kissed his way down her body, drinking in the soft taste of her skin and the husky rasp of her breathing and the strong arch of her back when he took each nipple into his mouth. When he palmed the curve of her belly and slid lower to part her thighs, she sucked in a ragged breath.

"You don't have to do that."

"Yeah, I do."

And he did. With tongue and lips, with a hunger long repressed, and when she tensed and cried out, when he felt her press down hard and start to come, he knew he had to be there. Now.

"Ready?" he asked, and for answer she arched her back and welcomed him inside with a low guttural sound that echoed through his chest and gut, all the way to the organ that drove down hard inside her.

Staggered by the power of his pleasure, he held himself still and rigid as he fought the urgent desire to keep on driving to an end. He was deep, all the way inside her climaxing body and her legs had wrapped around him, holding him tight against her.

"I'm always ready for you."

God, but that undid him. The thickness of her turned-on voice, the taste of her on his lips, the intensity he felt in her stillness as she watched him start to move. The way she rose to meet the drive of his body, thrust for thrust, flesh meeting flesh. The gentle caress of her fingers on his face and throat, and the not-so-gentle bite of her teeth when she came again without any warning. Against the heat of his skin, where chest and breast met and brushed and drove into hard contact again, he felt the cool brush of her necklace and his fingers twined around the chain and held on while the beast of desire swallowed him whole.

Head back, he took the last uncontrollable plunge and roared over the edge into completion.

Somehow Tomas managed to rouse himself before the lure of taking Angie again or letting her sleep in his arms took hold. And when he sat on the side of her bed and rubbed a hand over his face to clear the last traces of temptation from his consciousness, he realized that he held her A-letter necklace in his hand. In the last minutes of that wild ride he must have gripped her chain so hard that he broke a link.

He rubbed his thumb over the tiny charm and put it down on the bedside table. *A for aftermath, afterward, awkward.* The time to leave before he got comfortable in the lush folds of her sated body. *A,* he thought as he scooped up his clothes and retreated to his own bed, *for another night, another time, another chance at conception.*

Two more times and that was it. Done.

Then she was going home.

Angie heard the drone of a plane coming in from the west and her heart banked and rolled. In fact her whole body revved to instant Tomas-is-home, here-look-at-me! attention a good thirty seconds before logic kicked in. He hadn't said anything about flying anywhere...but then that didn't mean anything...more often than not he didn't say... and with so much acreage to get around, flying was an everyday feature of station life.

But she couldn't deny the punchy anticipation low in her stomach, the heaviness in her breasts, the tightness of her nipples. A little early, but Tomas was definitely home...almost. She shoved the last of the flowers she was arranging—until now, artfully—into the table centerpiece and dashed for the bathroom. No time for soaking in milky baths tonight. If he drove straight from the airstrip, no stops in-between, she had a maximum of ten minutes.

Hurry, hurry, hurry.

Shedding clothes along the way, she hit the shower running…then ducked straight back out for a shower-cap. No time for drying hair—she needed every precious minute for essentials. The red wine should be opened to breathe. Vegetables peeled. Cream whipped. For a wet, soapy second she rued letting the staff off early, again, so she could savor every detail of preparing and serving this special dinner.

An intense wave of nervous tension gripped her body. Ovulation day, she'd joked at breakfast this morning. *I'll make a celebratory dinner. Don't be late.*

It was a measure of the progress they'd made in twenty-four hours that she could joke about such a thing, even if neither of them had laughed. Even if his eyes had darkened and flared with unnamed emotion as they fastened on hers across the breakfast table.

Yes, they'd eaten breakfast together. The previous night they'd eaten dinner together, too, and he'd relaxed a tiny bit more, talking, smiling, even laughing at one of her anecdotes about Stink, the mechanic. For the second consecutive night he refused her offer to help with whatever office-work compelled his devotion, and she went to bed alone.

Around midnight he came to her room and made love with the same fierce power as the night before. Just once, damn him, and again he'd left her in the cooling sheets of her bed, hoping and wishing and praying that the next night might be different.

Well, Angie, the next night is about to begin.

Angie held her face tilted up for a last cool rinse and switched off the taps. *Last night, last chance.* She'd joked about this dinner but underneath, deep inside where her stomach was knotted with trepidation, she'd fastened her determination to make it special. A lot had changed in twenty-four hours, but not her conviction.

What had transpired between them in her bed the last two nights was too real, too huge, too intense, to cast aside as a purely physical joining. So many times she'd had to bite her tongue—or his shoulder—to stop herself blurting out what filled her heart. She'd curbed her natural inclination to tell it all, to lay it on the line, to charge ahead too fast.

She'd reined herself in and she would continue to do so.

Even when he asked her to go back to Sydney until she knew the result of this round of baby-sex—which she knew he would, probably tonight—she would keep it together. While preparing dinner, she'd also prepared her argument for staying and coached herself on delivering it with cool, direct logic.

If she failed, if he wouldn't listen to her reasoning, then at least she would get to experience something approximating a date. Tonight she wouldn't allow him to retreat to his work. Tonight they would walk hand in hand to bed. Tonight the light stayed on.

He owed her that much.

The dress she'd decided on earlier lay waiting on her bed. She traced one of the bright pink flowers and fingered the silky georgette material in momentary indecision. Too much? Probably, but in that second she heard the solitary bark of Tomas's heeler a second before the whole kennel joined in. A vehicle was coming.

Swallowing her hesitancy whole, she pulled the dress

over her head and wriggled until the satin lining shimmied its way over her hips and down to her knees.

"Hurry, hurry, hurry," she muttered. And of course the zipper stuck. She left it half-undone to shove her feet into white mules, to grab her brush and drag it through her moisture-messed hair…a task made easier when she remembered to take out her ponytail scrunchie. She slapped on some tinted moisturizer, glossed her lips, traced her eyes with kohl and smudged the lines.

Done!

She sucked in a quick breath…and realized she should be wearing a bra. If this were a real restaurant date, with other people present, she would take the extra minute to find one, to make some effort to disguise the hard jut of her nipples. But there were no other people…just her and Tomas and the fact that she couldn't think about him without this obvious result. Why hide that truth?

As she rushed to the living end of the house, she struggled to free the stuck zipper and strained her ears for the sound of his vehicle pulling up outside. She wanted to greet him at the door, to smile and say, "Hi, I missed you." To hand him his beer and, if she caught him really on the hop, surprise him with a kiss.

The canine chorus rose to a second crescendo as she entered the kitchen, then quieted immediately as if in response to a slash of the conductor's baton. Or a one-word command from their master. In the same instant—perhaps in response to the excited jump of her hand—the zipper released and glided effortlessly all the way to the top. That had to be a good omen, Angie decided.

She collected his beer and walked calmly to the door. Her heart, naturally, raced at a thousand miles an hour. That, she hoped, didn't show as clearly as her nipples.

Then she heard a vehicle pull up outside and her skin flushed with heat. The ice-cold bottle in her hand was suddenly very enticing. If she rolled it over her forehead, her throat, her breasts…

Tempting, but she didn't. Instead she drew a deep breath and walked out onto the veranda, lifting a hand to shield her eyes from the rays of the sinking sun. A car door slammed, then a second. Voices? The brief murmur was too far away to identify but it sounded like a brief exchange of words.

Lord, but she hoped the second was one of the mechanics who'd bummed a lift back from the airstrip and not a visitor. She cast a nervous glance downward. Yep, there they were. Both the girls still at full *hello-Tomas, boy-are-we-pleased-to-see-you* attention.

Okay, she was definitely going back to change. Except that decision had barely formed before the first figure walked into view—no *strode* into view—and it was not Tomas or any mechanic.

"Maura," she cried, nipples forgotten in a stunned blast of astonishment and joy. Back from the Killarney muster early and unexpected. And here at the homestead, not her own place.

Maura stopped, luckily, because that gave her a chance to brace herself before Angie hit at full speed. She wrapped her arms around Maura's reed-thin body and held on for all she was worth until her bubbles of surprised laughter turned to tears.

How did that happen? And why? Angie didn't burst into tears for no reason. She just…didn't.

A bit stunned, a lot embarrassed, she pulled back and attempted to gather herself.

"What's the matter, child?" Maura was frowning, her

expression a mixture of confusion and concern. "Why are you crying?"

"I don't know." She scrubbed harder at her face. "I think it's just the surprise of seeing you."

"Do I look so bad?"

Angie rolled watery eyes. In her youth Maura Carlisle had been a world-renowned model. In her mid-fifties, even her bad days couldn't hide that beauty. But before Angie could voice that opinion she glimpsed movement beyond Maura and her body stiffened reflexively.

Oh, no. She did not want to be caught crying. She was the strong, outback woman who would sail through the toughest days at his side.

But it wasn't Tomas who walked into her blurry wet-eyed field of vision, but Rafe. Her eyes widened…so did his, as they took in her dress, the bottle in her hand, the smudged kohl under her eyes.

"You're crying," he pointed out.

"I know that."

And if both Carlisles would stop looking at her so oddly she might be able to get some control over herself. Emotions and hormones and surprises and tears. Holy Henry Moses, she had to get a grip. She sucked in a breath, waved a hand in front of her face, and finally managed to halt the waterworks.

Rafe and his mother were still looking at her oddly.

"Nice dress," Rafe said.

"Is there a special occasion?" Maura asked. Then she turned on Rafe. "Did you know Angie was here?"

Oh, dear. Angie inhaled and wet her lips. "I just—"

"And when did you start drinking beer?"

"It's, um, not mine, actually."

"Speaking of which—" amusement, rich and redolent, colored Rafe's voice "—where is the man of the house?"

She flashed him a warning glance. "I wasn't expecting you. Either of you."

"Obviously."

Maura looked at him narrowly, then back at Angie. "Rafe flew out to visit me at Killarney. I had him bring me straight home when I heard the news."

Angie stiffened. "What news?"

"Alex has set a wedding date."

"In two weeks." Maura's lips came together in a disapproving line. "Civil vows in Melbourne! Why are they in such a rush? Alex fobbed me off with some cock-and-bull story about their busy lives. Rafe knows something and won't tell me. Do *you* know what's going on?"

Fixed with those straight blue eyes, Angie started to squirm.

Maura didn't miss that reaction. Her gaze narrowed. "Is Susannah pregnant? Is that what you're all trying to keep from me? "

"I don't know," Angie answered honestly, her gaze sliding away to Rafe's in silent appeal.

"Oh, for land's sake, will you two stop treating me like a fool! I know there's something going on with you all, not just Alex. I've been too wrapped up in myself since…" Her eyes sharpened, as if with remembered pain, but she drew a deep breath and continued. "Does this have anything to do with your father's will?"

Rafe rubbed at the back of his neck. Angie studied the bottle in her hand. Maura clicked her tongue in disapproval.

"I won't accept that. One of you is going to tell me the whole story and—"

"What story?"

Tomas? They all turned as one, three sets of eyes fixed on the new arrival. Angie felt her stomach drop as if a high-speed elevator had taken off and left her a nanosecond behind. Where had he arrived from? And why couldn't he have done so five minutes earlier?

His gaze slid from one to the other before settling on Angie. "What's going on?"

Ten

The dinner didn't unfold as it had done in Angie's imagination. While she attempted to stretch a meal-for-two four ways—she shouldn't have bothered, since no one had much of an appetite—Tomas and Rafe had drawn Maura a pretty thin sketch of the will clause. Angie knew it was sketchy by the questions Maura continued to ask after they'd all sat down for dinner.

They'd discussed Alex and Susannah and their no frills wedding. Maura, who'd given up all pretence of eating, supposed she wouldn't be able to do a thing to change her eldest son's mind. Silently Angie sympathized. Tomas was equally stubborn, when he made up his mind. And as for Rafe…

"What are you doing about this clause, Rafferty?"

Uh-oh. Maura used her sons' full names rarely. The upshot was always trouble. Angie put down her cutlery and started to collect plates—escaping to the kitchen and washing dishes suddenly looked very attractive.

"I'm still considering my options," Rafe said carefully.

"Of course you are." Maura's tone hovered between disgust and anger. "And what about you?" Her gaze speared Tomas. "Please tell me that's not why Angie's here."

The crockery in Angie's hands rattled its own answer, even after she gripped hard to stop the telltale clatter. She could feel Maura's eyes on her face, could feel the heat rising from her chest through her throat and into her cheeks. First tears and now she was blushing. What could she possibly do for a grand finale?

She knew what she wanted to do. She wanted to look this woman she loved like a mother right in the eye and tell her the truth. But she couldn't; she'd promised Tomas. Seated beside him at the table she could feel his tension even though he answered Maura's question with enviable composure. "I'll talk to you later, Mau. After we've—"

"Don't be ridiculous. We all know what's going on." Maura looked from one to the other, daring them to disagree. "Don't we?"

"It's no one's business but mine and Angie's. I'm not discussing it at this table."

For a long second the silence was chillingly complete, then Maura exhaled through her nose in a sound of pure exasperation. "If I'm reading your lack of denial and outrage correctly, you two are sleeping together to make a baby. Because Charles thinks—*thought*—he could make up for something that happened twenty-six years ago."

Angie put the stack of plates down with a loud clatter. Is that why Charles added this clause? To replace the baby his wife lost at childbirth? To make up for the devastation of that loss?

"We don't know that," Rafe said.

"No one knows why he attached that clause," Tomas added.

"I do," Maura said with more conviction than either of her sons. "I always wanted more children but after Cathy died, I couldn't, physically or mentally. Charles vowed he would make that up to me, that he'd make me happy again."

She shook her head slowly, sadly, and for the first time that night tears misted her vivid blue eyes. She hadn't been happy in a long, long time, Angie knew, but usually she maintained a stoic facade.

"You, child—" Maura pointed across the table at Angie. "You made me happy when you came to live here. You were such a wild, joyous little thing. So full of life and so eager to give these boys a kick in their arrogance."

"It was an easy target."

Maura's smile couldn't disguise the lingering sadness in her eyes. "And now you're making a baby with my son. Have you planned a wedding I know nothing about, too?"

"We're not getting married," Tomas answered, and his voice was about as tight as the constriction in Angie's chest.

"Even if a baby comes of this?"

"That's right."

Maura stared at her son a second longer, then shifted her attention one place to the left. "And is that all right with you, Angie?"

"Tomas was very straight with me," she said carefully, "about not wanting to marry again. I offered to have this baby, regardless."

Maura nodded once, accepting that answer even though she obviously didn't like it. Her disapproval and disappointment fisted hard around Angie's heart and squeezed with all its might. She longed to blurt out the truth, to say she wanted the marriage, the together, the forever, and she would probably keep on wanting it until the day she died. If she couldn't change the stubborn man's mind in the meantime.

"I'm not going to tell you how to live your life, Angie, that's not my place. But you know I was a single mother, twice over. I was lucky Charles came along and gave us all his love and this life and a complete family. I know which option I preferred, and that's all I have to say to you."

That's *all?* Lucky there was no more because Angie's poor heart would have caved. And the damn tears prickled the back of her throat so she couldn't even look Maura in the eye and say she knew what she was doing. Then she felt Tomas's hand on her knee, not a prolonged caress, but a single moment of pressure that expressed support and comfort and solidarity even.

It also made the battling-tears thing much, much worse.

"If you want to talk to me, Angelina," Maura said, pushing back her chair and getting up from the table, "you know where to find me."

"Thank you," Angie managed.

"Angie won't be staying much longer," Tomas said at the same time.

Maura paused, her gaze flicking from one to the other and obviously reading Angie's reaction correctly. "Charles and I told you a long time ago that this is your home," she said. "You stay as long as you want."

"I thought you were going to Wyndham today."

Angie's voice cut cleanly through the chill pre-dawn, catching Tomas midway through saddling his horse. His hands froze for a full second while his mind processed the facts. Angie. Out of bed. This early. At the barn. Carefully he finished cinching the girth before he turned to acknowledge her greeting. "I am."

"It's a long way on horseback."

Another time, after more sleep, he might have smiled at that comeback. Wyndham was a bloody long way by any transport other than plane. "I don't have to leave till eight. I'm riding out to Boolah first."

"Feel like some company?"

He hesitated—not to consider her request, but to decide how to put her off without a prolonged debate. After Maura's return and last night's dinner he knew they needed to talk, but not here, not yet. He hadn't slept more than an hour and as for Angie…

"You look like you should still be in bed."

"At this hour of the morning, *everyone* should still be in bed."

"Funny."

Except he didn't smile, not when she shifted her weight from one foot to the other and drew his attention to what she was wearing and not wearing. Like shoes. In fact, she looked like she'd rolled out of bed, tossed a denim jacket over her pajamas and raced from the house. And if her elevated breathing was anything to go by, she'd not only raced but sprinted the hundred yards from bedroom to barnside.

He gestured at the bare feet she was busy shuffling between. "Aren't you afraid you'll step in something fresh?"

"Funny." And she did manage a smile. "I heard you walk by my room and I was in a hurry to catch you before you left. For Wyndham. Since I thought that's where you were going." Her explanation started off jaunty and bright and then trailed off, as if she'd suddenly noticed his flat expression. At least that's what he was striving for. Flat, forbidding, go-back-to-bed-Angie.

"Sorry I woke you," he said, turning back to his horse and trying to recall where he'd left off with the saddle.

"Oh, you didn't. I was awake. Still."

"Yeah, well, after last night I don't imagine any of us slept well."

He heard her shift feet again, heard the soft exhale of her breath, and when he walked around his horse to check the offside he noticed that she'd started twisting her chain—the one he'd fixed for her yesterday—around her fingers. *A for aftermath.*

"It wasn't only what Maura said. I lay awake thinking you might come."

To her room? As he'd done the previous two nights?

Across his saddle their eyes met and held, sparking sudden heat into the chill morning air. For a long moment there was nothing between them but that heat and her honesty, and Tomas found he couldn't lie. "I thought about it," he said, moving back to his horse's head, gathering his reins. "Most of the night."

"But you didn't…because of what Maura said?"

His hands tensed on the reins and Ace tossed his head in protest. With a few soothing words, he rubbed the green colt's nose and promised to do better. For the horse, for his mother, for Angie who deserved much better than his recent treatment.

"I'm sorry she found out like that."

"Not as sorry as I am."

"It wasn't your fault," she said softly, and he sensed her coming closer, felt the way his body responded. "The will clause stated she wasn't to know."

"That doesn't make any of us feel a whole lot better."

"I know."

They stood in silence for several seconds, still but for the stroke of her hand on his horse's neck. That he could see from the corner of his eye, a long, slow, absent caress that made his own skin tighten. That made it remember every touch in the dark, every slow caress, every driving stroke of passion.

"I'm sorry, Angie," he found himself saying. "That first night in Sydney, you told me about the teenage crush. I knew you expected more from me than what I was prepared to give, but I didn't let it stop me. I should have. I'm sorry I've let you down."

"You haven't."

"Don't bullshit me. I know you wanted more these last nights."

Her hand stopped the idle stroking, and his horse whinnied a protest. Tomas sympathized. She had that effect, with her soft hands and warm eyes and easy touch. "It wasn't all bad," she said. "In fact some of it was pretty good. And I had plans for a spectacular last night."

"I noticed the dinner, the flowers, the candles. The dress." Especially the dress and the fact she'd not been wearing a bra. Same as now. When she lifted her hands to twist at her chain or rub at her arms—as she was doing now—he could see the dark outline of her nipples through the thin material of her pajama top.

"You liked the dress?"

Tomas swallowed. "Yeah." He liked.

A small smile touched her lips, a sweet and innocent contrast to the sultry heat in her eyes. "Maybe it's not too late. If you wanted to give this ride a miss and, well, you said you don't have to leave till eight."

Two hours. One last time. And it would be all about her, about what she liked, about her fulfillment. *A for atonement.* His body thickened in readiness; the air thickened with anticipation. And somewhere in the world beyond, a ringer whistled tunelessly as he approached the barn and the start of his working day.

"Mornin', boss," he said. Then, "Bit early for you, eh, Ange?"

He continued on his way, but his interruption hurtled Tomas back into the real world. *His* real world. "I think it best if we leave things as they are."

The hand at her throat stopped twisting the chain. "Do you mean altogether? Not try again at all, even if this time didn't work?"

"Yes. I do mean altogether," he said stiffly. He gave the girth one final check and excused himself so she stepped out of the way.

"Because Maura doesn't approve?"

He put his boot into the stirrup and looked her right in the eye. "Because Maura was right not to approve."

"But what about the inheritance?" She waved her arms wide. "What about all this? What about the ownership you've worked so hard for?"

"I've tried. It's up to Alex and Rafe now."

"Alex isn't married yet, and Rafe said he's still considering."

He swung into the saddle, adjusted his weight. "He's made up his mind…he's not telling Mau is all."

As intended, that news sidetracked her attention. She huffed out a breath. "Really?"

"Apparently he's going to ask her tomorrow night." He held up a hand, anticipating her next question. "Don't ask me. Ask him."

"I will, but I still won't believe it until I see it. I mean, Rafe as a father?"

"He never backs down from a challenge."

Her abstracted expression tightened and she looked up

at him sharply. "Is that what this is between you three? A challenge?"

"Not to me. Not to Alex. But to Rafe…probably. A challenge is the only thing that drives him." He gathered up his reins. "He's flying back to Sydney today."

"And you think I should go with him?"

"That's not my decision to make."

"I'm not staying if you want me gone," she said simply. "So it is your decision."

And what could he say? *Go, because I'm afraid to have you here. Go, before I can't walk past your door at night. Go, because I'm afraid of what you expect of me, afraid of what I can't give.*

"Stay until you know if you're pregnant. Then we'll both know."

"Well, Charlie, here we are then." Angie coaxed the elderly stock horse right up to the fence and sucked in a deep, dusty breath. "Wish me luck."

Being of the seen-it-all-before persuasion, Charlie didn't wish her anything that she could detect. In fact she thought the old darling might have nodded off around the three-mile mark and sleepwalked the rest of the trip. But he'd got her here, albeit slowly, and that was the main thing.

"Here" was the stockyards at Spinifex Bore, where Maura suggested she might find Tomas. And as she gathered up her reins and prepared to dismount, she cast her eyes over the cattleyard activity and zeroed in on his broad shoulders and tan hat instantly. Angie climbed from her saddle to the top rail without shifting her gaze from that tall, powerful figure standing right in the middle of the bellowing melee of cattle and dust and ringers. As always the sight of him turned her breathless, tight, hot in a dozen separate places, but as she watched him work the desire softened like candle wax before reshaping into a fuller, richer craving.

This was a man in his element, doing what he loved, what he was born for. This was her man, and this was the life she longed to live with him. Even through the pall of dust raised by a thousand milling hooves, nothing could have been clearer in Angie's eyes or mind.

It bolstered her resolve and reaffirmed her reason for riding out to see him today.

The notion had been simmering around in her brain for the five days since Maura's return, since the morning at the barn when he terminated their arrangement. In that time she'd caught occasional glimpses of the old Tomas, and the more she saw, the more she wanted that man back. Over and over she'd recalled her conversation with Rafe about coming out here.

He needs you more than he needs this baby, Ange. He needs you so he doesn't hole up in his shell like a hermit crab. That's why she'd come out here, and she was determined to do whatever she could with the little time remaining—not to get him back in her bed, but to remind him of the life he'd cut himself off from.

This morning Maura, unknowingly, handed her the perfect first step.

A slow smile spread across her face as she remembered her excitement as the plan took shape in her mind. As she recalled turning Maura's initial horrified, "Oh, no, child, no thank you," to nervous consent.

If Tomas approved.

Her smile wavered momentarily, but she forced it wider and lifted her chin. He would approve. She had her argument all worked out, an answer for every permutation of *no* she'd anticipated on the long, slow ride out here.

It was, simply, a flawless plan…and she'd been unable to sit around all day and wait.

"Moment of truth, sister," she muttered, and started to climb down into the action.

Tomas didn't see her arrival. What he saw was a jackaroo's distraction and a bullock charging at the draft. In one swift motion, he managed to push the kid aside and grab control of the gate.

"Shee-oot." The youngster dusted off his backside and cast a sheepish glance in Tomas's direction. "That was a close one."

"Unless you like hospitals, you don't even blink when you're working the draft. Understood?"

"Yes, boss."

Tomas nodded and handed control of the gate to the head stockman on this camp. "Watch him, Riley. I don't want any accidents."

"Then you better get the girl out of here."

Shee-oot.

He swung around and instantly saw the reason for, not one, but pretty much every ringer's distraction. Angie, wearing jeans that molded every inch of her backside, climbing into the yards. And smiling widely at every man who tipped his head and said "G'day, Ange." And paying scant regard or respect to the beasts in the yard.

What in the blue blazes did she think she was doing?

Jaw set in a heated mix of fury and fright for her safety, he strode in her direction. A few curt words set the men back on task. A few deep breaths brought his seething response under control.

Her smile faltered and dimmed when he caught her by the arm and swung her back into the relative protection of a corner. "What are you doing?" she asked, when he kept turning her until he was happy he could see both her and the cattle.

"I'm making sure you don't step into the path of half a ton of beef."

"I know what I'm doing." Eyes narrowed with indignation, she waved her free arm toward the activity. "I've been around cattle ten times as long as some of these kids."

"Then you should know this is the most dangerous place on the station. You shouldn't be distracting those kids."

She blinked slowly, and her gaze turned contrite. "You're right. I guess I should have waited up on the rail until you were done."

Tomas shook his head. Did she really think that sight wouldn't have distracted any red-blooded male? Her perched up there in her pretty pink shirt and tight jeans and Cuban heeled boots? His gaze narrowed on the footwear and then on the roping gloves that protected her hands. His gut tightened with a new and different fear. "Did you ride out here?"

"Of course I did. Why?"

He swore softly. Shoved his hat back from his brow. "What if you're pregnant?"

"I rode Charlie, not one of these bulls. I don't see how that could hurt." She looked perplexed, as if she didn't understand his concern. Hell, he didn't understand it completely. Not the almost irrational rush of terror when he imagined her galloping down here at the bone-rattling speed she'd favored in her youth.

"Charlie, huh." Readjusting his hat, he exhaled a long, slow draft of remnant fear. Charlie was a safer conveyance than anything on wheels. He'd overreacted, big time. "I can't imagine you enjoyed that much."

"He has two speeds—slow and slower. I swear that snails overtook us on the way out here." She smiled, but the softening of her expression kind of hitched in the middle when their eyes met and held. Still smiling, she reached out and touched his arm but her eyes were serious, dark, solemn. "I'll be careful, okay?"

That expression, that touch caught at his throat. He knew he'd have to clear it to speak, if he had anything to say, so he just nodded. And his gaze slid down to the warm pressure of her hand on his arm, not so much arousing as…unsettling. Because he wasn't thinking about those kid-gloved fingers stroking his bare skin. He wasn't thinking about them sliding down inside his jeans and folding around him. He huffed out a breath. He was thinking about them sliding down and folding around his hand and, hell, that's what he didn't understand.

And she must have misunderstood his intense interest in her touch, because she suddenly withdrew her hand and tucked it into the front pocket of her jeans. He had the weird feeling that she'd taken something from him and tucked it away.

Unsettling? Holy hell, yeah.

There was an uncomfortable passage of silence before Angie tipped the brim of her white hat and cleared her throat. "So," she said brightly, "do you want to hear why I put up with the slow ride all the way out here?"

Yeah, he did. But not here at the yards where she'd managed to turn him inside out with protective concern. With emotions he didn't want, didn't need, didn't understand. "You can tell me while I drive you back to the homestead."

"What about Charlie?"

"Riley can bring him home.

Her eyes narrowed with a frown, but Tomas didn't give her a chance to object. Yeah, he knew Charlie was old and slow and safe. But he also knew he couldn't go back to work knowing she was out there on horseback. Or still here at the yards with cattle milling around. Remnants of his earlier fear still twisted tight in his gut and sweated on his backbone. "This isn't debatable, Angie. I need to know you get home safely. You're riding in my ute."

Eleven

Angie was enjoying this protective concern of Tomas's a little too much, especially since she knew in her heart it was all about the baby—a baby she might not have conceived. And she really had wanted to spend some time at the yards, maybe even working the cattle alongside the ringers, as she'd done so many times in her teens. Another day, she promised herself. Today she had a more important agenda.

"So." Tomas glanced across at her from the driver's seat. "What's so important it couldn't wait until tonight?"

"Alex rang this morning. He and Susannah are coming out next weekend, to visit with your mother." A compromise, seeing as Maura—in fact, all of the family—would not be at their wedding. That's the way they wanted it, apparently. No fuss, low key, over and done. "Anyway, I was thinking it would be nice to invite a few neighbors over on Saturday night. The ones who've been here while you all grew up. Alex's friends."

"A party?"

"A very small one. Hardly a party at all, really, because Maura wouldn't come if there were too many people." Silently she apologized to Maura for using her obsessive dislike of crowds so shamelessly. "I thought it would be good for her, too, to see a few friends in a nonintimidating environment."

He made a sound that might have been agreement…or might not have. She snuck a quick peek at his face for reaction. None. Did he realize she was thinking that *he* needed to see a few people? To start mixing with *his* friends again?

"And in the interests of killing a few more birds with the one stone, I'd get to catch up with them, too. Before I leave." Deliberately she'd left that point till last. Since she rather thought the point about her leaving would score high points. She crossed all her fingers, metaphorically. "So, what do you think?"

"I think Mau won't have a bar of it."

"Well, you'd be wrong. She agreed…if you did."

He was silent for several long moments, his profile set in that obdurate fashion she knew so well.

"You won't have to do anything," she pressed. "Nor Maura. I'll do all the work."

"Bored with living out here already?" he asked.

The question sounded casual, like one of those by-the-way observations that can catch a person completely off guard. He didn't turn and look at her. His profile remained stern, hard, serious. And Angie's heart gave a warning bump. This was an important issue. She knew without knowing why…or perhaps she did know why.

Had Brooke grown tired of the outback life? Had she ever accepted the isolation? The absence of social stimulation, of shopping?

Not that she could ask, not when he'd cut her off so categorically the last time.

"Bored?" She laughed softly and shook her head. "I've never been bored out here. You know how keen I was to get back every school holiday."

"School was a long time ago. You've changed."

"Have I?" she asked, turning to face him, curious. "Because when I put on these jeans and boots I feel the same as I did back then."

"They're only clothes, Angie. Anyone can look the part."

"True, but I'm not playing a part, Tomas. I'm just me. The same old Angie."

"You're not the same, Angie. No more than I am."

"It's true that some things change or are colored by our experiences, but we're still the same here—" she tapped her chest, over her heart "—where it matters."

They'd pulled up outside the homestead and she knew she had to get out of the ute before she said too much about what was in her heart where it mattered, and how little had changed.

"Can you think about the party?" she asked as she opened her door. "Because I won't go ahead without your permission. Just think about it and let me know tonight, okay?"

In the dry season Tomas spent almost as much time away from home as at Kameruka Downs. That came with the Carlisle Cattle Company's growth and acquisition of stations and feedlots right across the north of Australia. He accepted the travel along with the management challenges, and compensated with as much hands-on cattle work as he could fit into his time on home territory.

This time he'd been gone three days and nights, a standard excursion to the Queensland fattening properties, nothing out of the ordinary. Yet as his plane dipped into its final approach to the Kameruka strip he felt much more than the usual dose of homecoming satisfaction. There was nothing standard about the powerful mixture of anticipation and anxiety that tightened his chest and gut.

That response owed nothing to the half-dozen station Cessnas parked alongside the strip, or the company plane that signified Alex's presence. Rafe was in America, allegedly on business—although Tomas suspected there was a woman involved. With Rafe there usually was.

No, Angie's party didn't excite him; seeing Angie again did. Too tired to muster the usual denial, he accepted the truth much the same as he'd accepted the done-deal with tonight's party.

How could he have said no to Angie's arguments? It might be his home, but this was a party for Alex and Susannah, for Maura, and for Angie.

As for Tomas…well, he had considered not turning up. It would have been easy to make a last-minute excuse so he could escape the speculation and covert looks and awkward pauses after someone spoke Brooke's name in a less-than-hushed tone. He hated all that. It was easier to avoid social functions—easier for him and easier for them.

As he taxied in he identified the various parked craft by their owners. All longtime neighbors and friends, so he'd have to be civil and spend at least a couple of hours in their company.

And after he hangared the plane and climbed into his ute, it struck him that their presence might actually have an up side. Already they were curbing an urgency in his blood, an impulse to flatten his foot and drive helter-skelter for home. If she were there alone—if she were waiting in the garden wearing a killer dress and a welcoming smile—he might do something stupid and foolhardy and ill advised.

A house full of visitors would curb those crazy-man homecoming urges. Alex's solid presence would remind him of the benefits of self-control. And Angie's presence... His heart pulsed hard in his chest with a sudden raw swell of nervous emotion.

Angie's presence would remind him of the date and the fact that today, tomorrow, the next day—one day very soon—they would know if she was pregnant or not.

The night was going about as well as Tomas had imagined. He went through the motions, talking to whichever of the guests cared to seek him out in his corner of the courtyard garden. Mostly they wanted to thank him for the invitation—apparently, *he'd* invited them!—and to congratulate him for handing the organization over to Angie.

Apparently she was a sensational hostess.

Ginger Hanrahan raved about her barbecue marinades. Di Lambert gushed about the fairy lights and asked if she could borrow them for her husband's surprise fortieth. "Surprise?" her husband muttered. "The only surprise is that none of you Carlisles has snapped up Angie. Are you all blind?"

No, Tomas wasn't blind. He could see that Angie wore the same dress as the night of their aborted dinner...except tonight she wore a bra. The tiny ivory one he'd scooped up from his bed the day she arrived, he discerned, since every time she leaned over the buffet table he caught a glimpse of one delicate satin strap.

It was driving him mad, the dress and the peekaboo strap and the fact that he couldn't stop watching her.

"Knockout dress," Alex said at his side.

Tomas scowled, not because Alex had noticed The Dress—who hadn't?—but because he'd noticed Tomas noticing The Dress. Continuously. He had to stop staring.

"Enjoying your party?" he asked his brother.

"Tolerably."

Tomas lifted a curious brow at that answer.

"We only agreed to come for Mau's sake," Alex said. "We didn't need a party."

Tomas's silence was empathetic, since he didn't need a party, either. His gaze scanned the several small groups, found Angie, of course, but not Alex's fiancée. "Where's Susannah?"

"Gone to bed."

"Already?"

"Headache."

Which explained why she'd looked so pale and tense, he supposed, although to his mind Susannah never looked anything else. His gaze slid back to Angie, Susannah's vibrant, strong antithesis. She was talking to David Bryant, her head tilted as she listened intently, and in the muted garden light she practically glowed. For a second he was struck breathless by her sultry beauty, and then by his unconscious description.

His heart thudded hard in his chest. Was that the pregnancy thing they talked about? That inner glow?

At two weeks? Yeah, right. More likely it was the reflection off her party lights and the heady excitement of mixing with other people, new people, party people like herself.

He turned his head and looked away, and when Alex wandered off to check on Susannah, he found a shadowy corner where he couldn't see Angie. She could talk till she was blue in the face about loving this place and this life, but what she loved was people. Lots of people and stimulation and conversation. She wouldn't be any happier living here than Brooke, not once the honeymoon was over.

That word choice settled hard in his gut. What was he doing comparing Angie with Brooke? And talking about honeymoons? He'd definitely had too long a day; he needed sleep. But as he stood glowering in the shadows, wondering how quickly he could execute a round of farewells, music started up in the great-room that opened onto the courtyard.

A few couples took to an arbitrary dance floor and he knew he'd missed his moment for a quick leave-taking. He watched the dancers, drawn by the image of coupledom and unable to look away. He watched their hands connect and their bodies brush, saw their shared smiles and moments of eye-meet, and felt a restless emotion swell inside him, a pain he didn't want to name or know. A loneliness he thought he'd learned to control.

Abruptly he turned to leave, and swung right into Angie.

"Hey, I've been looking for you." And she had, for most of the night. Covertly watching, noticing how he always stood a little apart, how he never seemed to relax or laugh or embrace the party spirit. How at times he watched her with a quiet intensity. How at others he looked as remote and inaccessible as his Territory home.

Now she looked up into his darkly shadowed face and realized that his expression wasn't flat and remote. At close quarters his eyes burned with a harsh blue light, a wildly ambiguous mix of yearning and heat and restraint that reached inside and fisted around her heart. Had she actually thought that throwing a party and forcing him to mix with a few old friends would somehow ease his inner torment? She was such an idiot. Such a Pollyannaish, rosy-glass-wearing fool.

"I'm sorry," she breathed, a hoarse whisper that sounded as dark and intense as the moment.

"Sorry? For what?"

How could she say for everything? All the things she longed to change and for not knowing how or where to start? She huffed out a breath, jerked her head toward the partygoers. "For making you endure this. It hasn't been much fun, has it?"

"I've never been much for parties," he said. "Don't judge this one's success by me. You did a great job."

Yes, right, and she knew that. She knew the party had been a big success for the neighbors who still danced and talked and laughed, and a milder success for Alex and Susannah and Maura. But she'd wanted so much more from this evening. More of the impossible, she supposed, as always seemed to be the case with Tomas.

She looked away, off at the dancers who were moving in sinuous rhythm to a slow, torchy soul number. She'd deliberately chosen this song for tonight's mix, thinking to get him on the dance floor. Thinking to wind her arms around his neck and to nestle against his shoulder and to brush knees and thighs and bodies. It was a song for lovers to dance to, to undress to, to make love to with the same sizzling beat.

So, sister, why are you standing here dying with wanting? Why don't you take his hand and coax him onto the dance floor? Isn't that why you sought him out?

"So." He cleared his throat, and turned at the same time as Angie. Their hands collided in a brush of heat that singed the words on her tongue. For a moment they stood staring at each other, all burning eyes and dark heat and electric want. She didn't imagine it. It was there, blue fire in his eyes, the only impetus she needed.

She tilted her head toward the music. "Do you realize we've never danced together?"

Heat flickered in his eyes, heat and a note of restraint. "I don't dance, Angie."

"Never? Or just with me?"

He didn't answer.

"Come on, Tomas, humor me. I chose this music specially and I—"

"Leave it alone, Angie," he said harshly. "I'm not dancing with you."

"Because you don't want to touch me? Or because you do want to?"

Acknowledgment, hot, strong, direct, charged the air as their gazes met and held. Angie's whole body swelled with the unspoken but conceded knowledge—he wanted her. He might not like it, he might deny it tomorrow, but tonight he wanted her. She watched his nostrils flare slightly, watched the almost visible pull of restraint as he gathered himself, as he prepared to speak.

To tell her it made no difference. To call it sex, desire, lust. To say—

"Either of you care to join me for a nightcap?"

Alex. Angie sucked in a breath and prepared to tell him that, for an organizational genius, his timing sucked. But Tomas was already accepting the invitation to escape. Angie let her breath go and shook her head. "No, not me."

When Alex headed back in search of a decent port, Tomas hesitated a moment. "I'll see you tomorrow. At breakfast."

Angie sensed this was more than a casual comment, but she was riding too fine a line between frustration and annoyance to pay more heed. "Sooner," she said shortly. "In all probability."

He tensed in a most satisfying way. "Sooner than breakfast?"

"I'm going to need to use your bathroom at some point. If that's all right."

"Come on, Angie, stop playing games." A muscle ticked in his jaw, and she couldn't tell if that was about tension or fear or just plain annoyance. "Tell me what the hell you're talking about."

"It's a long story, but—"

"Give me the short version."

Yes, he was definitely annoyed. And for some reason Angie felt her own irritation diminish exponentially. With a soft, relenting sigh, she gave him the short version of her one organizational blunder. "I miscounted overnight guests and came up one bed short, so I'm sleeping on the sofa in your office. Your bathroom's closest and will be least congested."

He stared at her. The muscle in his jaw clenched and released again. "Have my bedroom. I'll take the office."

"Oh, no, you can't do that." Angie shook her head with some determination. "The sofa's not that long."

"By the time I get there, I'll be ready to sleep anywhere."

She saw that now, the tiredness in his eyes and posture. She heard the weariness in his voice, and both combined to steal the last of her irritation. "If you're tired enough to sleep anywhere, why not your bed?"

"I told you—it's yours."

"It's a big bed," she said evenly. "Why don't we just share it?"

Twelve

Good going, Angie. You didn't provide the fun, relaxing meet-with-friends that would change Tomas's attitude to life and love and laughter. You didn't get your slow dance in his arms. You didn't even get close to a hand-in-hand walk to his bedroom. And—to end the night on a perfect note—you chased him from his bed.

For about the fiftieth time since she climbed into that bed, Angie rolled over and checked the bedside clock. Three o'clock. He couldn't still be nightcapping with Alex, surely. She pictured his six-foot frame curled up and hell-ishly uncomfortable on the five-foot sofa and growled with frustration.

She should be the one tossing and turning on the sofa, not in his king-size bed. That's what she'd intended all along. Sure, she'd started the whole who-sleeps-where exchange in provocative fashion. But only because he'd grabbed such a quick hold of Alex's convenient escape hatch.

Nightcap, Tomas? Does this mean I get out of answering Angie's question about why I won't dance with her? Oh, yeah, I'm there!

"Because you do want to touch me," she murmured. "Why is that so damnably bad?"

With another prolonged growl, she covered her face with her hands and remembered the heat, the knowledge, the breathless pounding swell of certainty. And for a second she thought the growl continued, like a deep echo of the frustrated wanting that reverberated through her. But, no, it was voices in the hallway outside, and her whole body tensed in silent, hopeful wait.

The door opened, and in the slice of light from the hallway she saw his silhouette, tall and dark and hesitant. Should she feign sleep? Would that make up his mind?

"I'm not asleep," she said, too wound-up to fake anything for long. "You can turn on the light if you want."

He didn't, but at least he came the rest of the way into the room and shut the door behind him. Angie closed her eyes briefly and murmured a quiet thank you. "I'd decided you must have crashed on the sofa, and I was lying here thinking—"

"Go to sleep, Angie."

The mattress dipped as he sat on the far side of the bed, a long, long way from Angie. She rolled onto her side and propped herself up on one elbow. It took a second for her eyes to adjust, to find his outline in the dark, to identify the movements of his arms as he tugged off his tie. Unbuttoned his shirt. Stripped it off.

Angie swallowed. Cleared her throat. Tried to think of something to say, an excuse to be sitting here watching him undress. "I can't go to sleep. Not until I'm sure you don't think this is some kind of setup."

"A setup?"

"A ploy to get into your bed."

"Alex told me what happened with the Hanrahans bringing that extra couple." He leaned over, she imagined to take off his shoes. "You don't have to explain."

"So we're good with this—with sharing the bed?"

He'd gone still, the set of his shoulders tense and Angie thought he might have shaken his head. Just one small, disbelieving movement before he answered. "Yes, we're good. Can we leave it?"

Not waiting for her answer, he stood abruptly, undid his trousers, kicked them off. Desire speared through Angie, a strong, sweet ache that came of knowing he stood so close in nothing but his underwear. Would he climb into bed now? Would she be able to stand to lie here, to not reach out and touch?

But he started to walk away and struck by momentary panic, she bolted upright. "Where are you going? I thought you were good with sharing."

He stopped and his sigh sounded unnaturally heavy in the darkness. "I'm not that good with it, okay? I'm taking a shower and I could be a while, so just go to sleep."

He was gone longer than Angie would classify as "a while," but how could she sleep? Through the bathroom door she could hear the sounds of his shower, and when she shut her eyes she saw him in that split second before he closed the door. Illuminated by the bathroom light, in tall, tense, erect profile.

Was that why he said he would be a while? Did he need to take care of that hardness? Did he mean to cure it with a cold-water blast or ease it with a warm, soapy hand?

Heat washed through her, heat and a dangerously alluring temptation. What would he do if she walked into the bathroom and into the relentless wet pounding of that shower? Would he welcome her initiative, her hand, her body?

Hot and restless, she kicked the sheet from her body but the still bedroom air felt no less sultry. Even her silky little nightdress felt too much against her overheated skin. She sat up. Stared at the door. Started to peel the straps from her arms.

I don't like surprises.

Life was so much easier as an impulsive, straight-forward, do-what-comes-naturally gal. Before he filled her mind with doubts and insecurities and cause for caution. She hated diffidence. She loathed this whole game of patience. She despised hiding her feelings, her wants, her heart's desire.

"Aargh." Arms and legs akimbo, she flung herself back onto the bed, kicked the sheet further away, pummeled the pillow. And about a second after she jammed her eyes shut, she heard the blessed silence of a shut-down shower. Probably she took a number of breaths in the ensuing minute or two. That seemed likely since she didn't pass out from oxygen deprivation. But Angie didn't remember doing anything other than lying in heart-thumping stillness.

Waiting.

He came out of the bathroom naked, but not to the bed. After he walked out of her line of vision she heard the soft shush of a drawer rolling open, and she wondered what he was pulling on. The fitted briefs he wore so well. Sleep-shorts. Full body armor.

Too tense for amusement at that last image, she closed her eyes and smoothed her nightdress down over her body. He didn't like surprises. And despite the eyes shut and his silent barefoot approach, she knew exactly when he arrived at the bed. She knew he stood looking down at her.

"It's okay," she said, a husky sliver of sound in the dark. "I won't bite."

Ah, but she did. The heat of her voice. The shimmer of her nightdress. The line of her legs against his pale sheets. They all bit great ravaging holes in Tomas's willpower, in everything he'd convinced himself to avoid in that shower. And while he stood there with all his blood and willpower and logic racing south, she stretched out her arm and ran a hand across the sheet.

"See…I can't even reach your side."

Apparently that was a demonstration of his safety. Laughable, really, given the perilous snarling state of his body. She might as well have reached over and ran that hand over his butt. He sat that part of his anatomy down on the edge of the mattress and considered the alternatives. Sheet or no sheet? Tent or no tent?

"Did the shower help?" she asked.

And this time he did laugh, a caustic, rough-edged sound that had little to do with amusement and a lot to do with the timing of her question. "Not my immediate problem, no." However, he was very, very clean.

"Hot or cold?"

What? He swung his legs onto the bed, kept them bent, pulled up the sheet hip-high.

"The unhelpful shower," she persisted. "Was it hot or cold?"

He rolled his head a little on the pillow, enjoying the cool imprint of his wet hair. It was the only hint of coolness in his burning body. "Do you really expect me to answer that?"

"It would stop me wondering."

Yeah, well, maybe it would. And just maybe it would shock her into silence. "I tried both. Neither worked."

"Does it usually?" Her silence had lasted all of ten seconds. And she didn't sound very shocked…just curious. "The cold method, I mean. I'm well aware that the, um, hot alternative does its job."

"You know this from experience?"

"More from reading than firsthand." She huffed out a little sound of amusement. "No pun intended."

"None taken."

He heard her move, a silky frisson of movement as she turned or shifted positions. And, hell, he could feel her watching him. Intently. Which didn't exactly help the problem they were discussing.

"You still haven't answered my question."

Shee-sus. "If you want to know how I get off, why don't you just ask instead of beating around the bush."

"Interesting phrasing," she said after the briefest pause. "But that wasn't really my question. I asked if cold showers help."

"Sometimes. Other times, you need a release."

She didn't say anything for a long while, so long that he thought he'd finally satisfied her curiosity. Long enough that he turned his head on the pillow to check. He wished he hadn't. She lay on her side, closer to the middle of the bed than he would have liked, just watching him with a quiet intensity that grabbed him in more places than under the carefully draped sheet.

"Is that satisfying?"

He made a strangled sound, part disbelief, part laughter. "Jeez, Angie. Can't you just read about this in a magazine?"

"I'm asking *you,* Tomas. I want to know if there's a difference between that kind of release and making love with a woman."

"Of course it's better with a woman."

"With any woman? Like one you pick up in a bar or something?"

"I wouldn't know."

Angie was so involved in her side of the conversation, in choosing her careful words to keep him talking, sharing, giving, that his answer took a moment to sink in. She frowned. "What do you mean?"

"I mean, I haven't slept with a lot of women."

"I didn't think that you had, actually."

"My inexperience showed?"

"No." Surprised by his question—by its tone—she lifted up on her elbow, better to see his face. "Why on earth would you say that?"

"Two, okay? You and Brooke. Is that what you wanted to know?"

"I..." God, what could she say? Angie wet her dry mouth but that didn't help when she had no words.

"Have I finally managed to shock you?"

Not shocked, she realized as the impact of his honesty took hold, but blown away that he'd told her. "It doesn't surprise me," she said slowly. "Knowing the kind of man you are... No, I'm not shocked."

"You don't know me, Angie."

"I've known you most of my life, Tomas. I know what matters to you. I know that you never looked at another woman once you met Brooke. I know this whole deal with me and the baby has been incredibly difficult because you still love her—and because you could never treat sex casually."

She could feel his tension radiating across the space that separated them in the big bed, could sense the barriers going up, but Angie couldn't stop. He'd shared something incredibly personal, and she wanted—no, *needed*—to do the same.

"If your inexperience showed, then I wouldn't have noticed. Every time I slept with you, every time you came to my bed and every time you came in my body, was completely amazing. Completely."

There. She'd said it. And as much as the words, she heard the resonance of her heartfelt passion filling the heavy silence of afterward, perhaps because her heart and her body were so jam-packed with love and need and wanting that she could no longer contain it all.

"Do you know yet?" he asked.

Instantly, with absolute certainty, she knew what he meant. Her heart bumped hard against her ribs and she felt its beat low in her body, deep in her womb. "I don't have my period yet, but that doesn't mean anything necessarily. Not yet."

"When?"

"Maybe tomorrow, although…"

When her voice trailed off he turned his head sharply, his eyes piercingly intense in the dark. "Although?"

"I don't feel PMSy, either." She laughed, a soft nervous bubble of sound, because he'd forced her to think about the forbidden. Every thought and connection she'd disallowed herself these past few days. "No chocolate cravings. No bloated tummy. I feel…"

She pressed the palm of one hand against her stomach, and felt an overpowering surge of emotion, part awe, part excitement, part nerves. Was she pregnant? Was there a minute speck of life already dividing and growing beneath her hand?

"How do you feel?" he asked, his voice low and gruff.

How did she feel? As if she hovered on the brink of something momentous. As if the night and their tenuous connection rested on her answer and his response. Her heart thudded so hard she felt constricted and breathless, and the arm holding her weight suddenly wobbled and wavered.

Before it collapsed her gracelessly, she sank down onto the bed and rolled onto her back. And she could find only one word to sum up that crushing wave of emotion. "Terrified."

"Of having the baby?"

"I'm more terrified that I'm overreacting and overreading these tiny little signs."

Slowly she turned her head and saw his eyes slide down her body. Everywhere they touched she felt an acute need, a cry from deep in her heart, and when they came to rest on her stomach, she could take no more.

"I'm more terrified," she said huskily, reaching for his hand and drawing it to her, "that there is no baby here." She pressed his hand against the curve of her belly. "I'm afraid that if I'm not pregnant I will leave here next week and that will be it. Over between us."

She stroked her fingers between his, linking them, letting him know with her eyes and the arch of her body how much she craved his touch. "One more night," she whispered. "One more time."

"That won't help anything, Angie." Their gazes locked in a clash of heat and resistance, as he dragged his hand free and back to his side of the bed.

Angie followed. Slowly, inexorably, she peeled the sheet from his body and she touched him with only her fingertips, a teasing stroke as soft as he was hard. Breath held, she waited, knowing the night's outcome hovered on the brink of this second.

He didn't move. He didn't turn. He didn't run. And when she pressed her palm against him, when she molded her fingers to his thick heat, his whole body shuddered in response.

"I can help you with what the shower couldn't," she whispered. "Let me."

His eyes burned into hers as she leaned in to kiss his mouth, and when their tongues came together in a slow, wet slide of heat the last threads of his resistance gave. She saw the flames leap, felt them spark and take hold in her body. She kissed him and caressed him until their breathing grew ragged and then she slid down his body, kissing him in a dozen quick places as she went.

She paused below his waist and told him she'd wondered.

"About what?"

"What you put on." From hip to hip, she traced the wide black band at the top of his fitted boxers. "When you came out of the shower."

"Would you like me to take them off?"

"No." She dipped her hand into the waistband. "I would like to take them off."

He helped her by lifting his hips. She didn't help him by scraping her nails down his thighs. Or by dipping down and pressing her lips to the satiny tip of his erection. Then she eased back and took him in her hand.

"I was thinking about this, all the time you were in that shower."

"So was I." His voice was a low, hoarse rip of breath.

"I wanted to touch you, here—" she slowly stroked the full slick length "—and here."

She moved lower and cupped his heavy weight, squeezed gently until he groaned in a mixture of pleasure and protest.

"And not only with my hand."

His eyes flashed with dark heat. "No."

"You don't want me to make love to you?" She shifted closer, until her hair settled in a dark cloud over his tight belly, then she turned her head and rubbed her cheek against him, a soft sensual caress that filled her with a shivery tension.

She touched him with her tongue and his stomach muscles clenched as he sucked in quick air. And when she took him into her mouth and tasted him with slow, moist pressure he swore softly and profoundly and it wasn't in protest. His hands fisted in her hair, stroked her face, touched her lips where they touched him, and his whole body jolted.

"Not like this," he said, as tight and hard and strained as his body. "Inside you."

Fingers fisted in her satin slip, he dragged her up to his mouth and kissed her deep, fierce, long. In the whisper of a moment he stripped her bare, but when he started to ease her onto her back Angie resisted.

"Not like that." Hands planted on his shoulders, she forced him back down. "This time, I'm making love to you."

When she came up on her knees and straddled him, hot hands spanned her waist and stroked around and over her bottom. In a hard roll of flexed muscles, he rose up from his waist to lick across her nipples, one after the over. To draw at her breasts until she cried out with a greedy need for more, for now, for him in her body.

"Now?" Raw, guttural, hot. "Here?"

And he parted her, stroked her there, found her wet and wanting. His eyes burned with the same blue fire that lit her blood as she lowered her hips and took him inside, and her heart all but exploded with the immensity of joyful hope.

This was different. This wasn't a quick, purposeful joining in the dark. This wasn't about making babies.

In this position there was no hiding. Their eyes locked and held with a connection more intimate than the slow, luscious slide of her body on his. More intense than the fire that licked at her control as he lifted and thrust hard. Fiercer than the heat whirling and spiraling through her blood as she rode him harder and faster until the climax exploded in a searing incandescent flash.

And tonight he wasn't leaving afterward. Angie collapsed in his arms and listened to the strong race of his heartbeat against her cheek until sleep claimed her.

Angie woke alone, but that didn't dim her memory of the night or of sleeping in her lover's arms. Her lover, her man, her love. A goofy big smile spread across her face as she smoothed a hand over the tangled sheets. Cool, but that didn't faze her blissful state.

Tomas always woke early, Sunday or not. Usually he rode, although some days he spent the early hours in his office. Today he'd been awake before dawn, when she'd needed the bathroom. Awake but not yet up, and when she'd returned to the bed he'd drawn her into his body, spoonlike, and cradled her belly with a protective tenderness that had twined her heart even faster to his.

Her hand crept now to that same spot, and a thrill of nervous excitement shivered through her body. She had to be pregnant. She felt too changed to be anything but. Not different physically—she palmed the rounded curve that was her normal shape—but different as a woman. Hormonally, she thought, and she smiled even wider, amused with herself.

Could she really recognize the different mix of hormones at play? Could she know without knowing?

Slowly she turned her head on the pillow and her eyes fastened on the bag sitting by the bathroom door. The bag she'd hastily packed with what she might need overnight and what she didn't want visitors to unwittingly find in her room. Things such as the half-dozen pregnancy test kits she'd brought with her from Sydney.

Her heart thumped hard in her chest. Too early? Maybe, maybe not. The instructions said the test was accurate from the time of a missed period, but was she missing a period yet? Maybe, maybe not.

She swung her legs over the side of the bed and slowly padded toward the bag.

Thirteen

Tomas's early morning ride wasn't an easy lope to check water or the recently weaned herd, but a testing session with his young colt. Ace was ready to step up his training and as for Tomas—well, he needed an activity that required concentration, something to ground him in his world, to settle the niggling sense that giving in to Angie last night had changed everything.

It hadn't. A weak moment and consensual sex without promises altered nothing. If anything had changed, then it was down to his visits to her bed two weeks before.

If.

The little word wormed its disturbing way into his composure as he strode back to the homestead. If she was pregnant. If she decided she wanted to stay. If he couldn't convince her he had nothing more than his body to give.

He circled around the back, avoiding the living area

where the overnight guests would be gathering for breakfast. He would do his duty and join them, but first he needed to shower and change. Outside his bedroom door he hesitated a moment. His pulse hiked, and he hated that uncontrolled response as much as he hated his indecisiveness.

And all for nothing, because he opened the door to an empty room. The bed was made, her overnight bag gone, and he fought an illogical sense of letdown. He'd dreaded this morning meeting and what she would say, what she might expect of him, the questions she hadn't asked in the night that he knew she wouldn't let lie.

God, had he really told her he'd only ever been with one woman, his wife?

Shaking his head, he crossed toward the bathroom, undoing his shirt as he went. He'd started to reach for the doorknob when he heard a sound beyond and stopped short.

The door opened and Angie made a soft noise of surprise and took a quick step back. She looked caught-out, and that made no sense at all. Nor did her husky-voiced apology.

Tomas frowned. "Sorry for what?"

"For…" Her brows drew together and her hand came up to fidget with her chain. *A for anxious.* "Because I'm still here. Using your bathroom."

"You asked if you could use it last night."

"And I should have been gone by now, with the guests and breakfast and all."

She was dressed, clinging to her bag with a white-knuckled grip, not quite meeting his eyes. There was something wrong—completely wrong—with this picture. He glanced beyond her for clues, and it struck him with sudden clarity.

The bathroom.

"Have you got your period?"

Her eyes widened and, to his horror, filled with moisture. Damn, but he'd rather face a ton of enraged cleanskin bull than a woman in tears. Especially a woman like Angie, whose tears always meant something.

Out of his depth, floundering with what to do, what to say, he took the bag from her hand and put it down outside the door. "Hey," he said gently, awkwardly. "It's okay."

"Don't." She sucked in a shaky breath, thick with those brimming tears. "You're only making it worse."

"Making what worse?"

"This. Tears. Bloody hormones." She made a low growly sound in her throat, a sound of struggle and exasperation that kicked him hard in the gut like that ton of cleanskin bull. And when he reached for her, when his hands closed over her shoulders, she walked into his chest and buried her face under his chin.

Being Angie, she didn't just let go and cry. Her breath rasped hard as she struggled for control. Her shoulders were stiff with her inner battle and he smoothed his hands over them, rubbed her back, stroked her hair and shifted his feet because he was uncomfortable in too many ways. She sniffed a wet apology, then rubbed at the moisture with the flat of her hand.

"If that's supposed to be a mop up," he murmured, "it's not helping."

"A shirt would have helped."

With one hand he shrugged out of his undone shirt and shoved it into her hand. "There you go."

A laugh hiccupped through her tears, but she took it and used it to mop at his chest. For too long. His body's response was completely inappropriate, entirely male, irrationally intense. And the only way he could deal with it was by remembering what had started this.

"You ready to answer my question yet?"

Her gaze snapped to his, wide-eyed and still bright from the tear-storm. She swallowed, moistened her lips, but then answered with a quick shake of her head.

"No, you're not ready or no, you haven't?"

Her gaze fell away, down to where her fingers clutched tightly at the balled-up shirt in her hands. Probably answer enough, but Tomas needed to be sure. With a finger under her chin, he tipped her face back up.

"Tell me, Angie."

"No, I haven't," she said, and something uncoiled deep in his gut. He didn't want to call it relief, didn't want to call it anything but concern for her and whatever had caused this outburst of emotion. "Then what was all this about?"

"I did a test this morning." She straightened her shoulders and met his eyes. "It was negative."

"Isn't it too early to be accurate?"

"I should have left it a couple more days, to be sure, but I couldn't."

"Impatient as ever?"

"I wanted to know."

Yeah, he could see that in her glistening eyes. He could hear it in the wobble in her voice. She wanted to know and she wanted the result to be positive.

Looking at her face now, he remembered in the night when she'd placed his hand on her belly, remembered the sensations roaring through his body, too many, too fast, too intense. Remembered fighting his way out of that drowning sensation and his relief when she'd reached out and touched him. When his responses turned primal, sexual, elemental. That he could understand and deal with, but not the undertow of emotion he saw in her eyes now. Reaching out, dragging him down to a place he never wanted to go again.

"I so wanted—"

He touched her mouth with his thumb. "Be patient, Angie. You said yourself it might be too early. Do you have another test kit?"

"Several."

"But you'll wait two days before you do another?"

She sighed softly. "Two days. Okay. I will."

When Tomas had to leave the next day on an overnight trip to his western-most station, he almost invited Angie along. A distraction, he'd thought, so she wouldn't run through those several test kits one after the other. He thought about her traveling beside him in the plane, thought about her sharing his bed, thought about her company and the interest she was taking in his business.

Thought about being with her when she read that test result, when her eyes looked up at his, all dark and luminous with—

No. He shut the gate on that thought-track with brutal speed. And he flew west alone, the way he was used to, the way he liked it, the way it would always be.

Thirty-six hours later he returned the same way.

By now she would know. He didn't let himself imagine one outcome or the other, didn't allow himself anything other than an urgency to find her and to know the result. By the time he tracked her down at the waterhole, his edginess had escalated to an acute tension that held his backbone and shoulder muscles rigidly straight.

"Mau said I'd find you here." A fitting location, the waterhole, seeing as this is where it all started. Where she'd looked him in the eye and said she would have his baby.

Today, however, her eyes were fixed on the surface of the water that glistened gold in the late-afternoon sun.

"Did she tell you about Rafe?"

"Getting married? Yup." He hadn't wanted to talk about his brother's out-of-nowhere Vegas wedding with Mau, and he sure as hell didn't want to discuss it now.

He squatted down beside her, intent on telling her so until she slanted him a guarded look across her shoulder. "The pressure's off then. With Alex's wedding next week and now Rafe doing his bit."

Tomas went completely still. "What are you saying, Angie? Yes or no?"

"I don't know. I still don't have my period, but the second test was negative." Tomas swore softly, and she huffed out a breath. "My sentiment exactly."

"Are these home tests reliable?"

"I don't know. I've never had cause to use one before."

He stared at her a moment, unsure what to make of her frame of mind. "What now?" he asked.

"I suppose I'll have to see a doctor."

"You don't sound very happy about the prospect." In fact she sounded downright reluctant, and that rubbed the rough edges of his mood. "What if there's something wrong? You said yourself your cycle is regular—" his eyes narrowed "—or was that a stretch of the truth?"

"Is that what you think?"

"No." He let his breath go on a relenting sigh. "No, I don't. You sounded so…reluctant."

And he sounded so worried that Angie's umbrage turned to instant mush. "I'm fine. Really, I am."

"Is there a doctor in Sydney you'd prefer to see?" he asked, obviously unconvinced.

"Not really, but—"

"I'll ring Alex tonight. He'll know someone."

"You think Alex sees a gyno?"

Not the right time for making jokes, Angie decided as she watched his mouth set in a tight line. But she'd felt the need to grasp at something, anything—including bad humor—before the decision about her immediate future and everything she longed for slipped away.

Okay. No more jokes, no more evading. Moment of truth, sister.

Drawing a deep breath, she slowly turned her head and looked into his eyes. Flat, hard, unyielding. Her heart skipped. "I'm not reluctant about seeing a doctor. I do want to know what's going on. I want to *know.*"

"What is the problem then?"

"I don't know that I'm ready to leave here."

"That's what we agreed, Angie."

And if she was leaving, if this was over, then why hold back? She had nothing to lose in laying everything bare, everything she'd struggled to hold inside these last weeks. Everything that brimmed in her heart.

"That's what we agreed—" she said softly "—before we made love the other night."

Something flared in his eyes for a split second before he set his jaw in that stubborn, uncompromising line. But that minute reaction was enough to set Angie's resolve to match. *Oh, no, Tomas Carlisle. It's time to stop hiding. It's time to find out what you really think.*

"At least that's what I did. I made love to you, with my body and my heart and my soul." Resistance, strong and hard flattened his expression and she leaned closer, placed her hand on his arm. "I'm sorry if you don't want to hear this, but I need to tell you. I can't *not* tell you."

"I didn't promise you anything," he said tightly.

"Oh, I know that. You never promised me anything way back when I fell in love with you, either, but that didn't stop me."

"You were a kid."

"I was eighteen and grown up enough to know what I wanted. That's never changed, Tomas. I've loved you a long time—probably forever—but it really hit hard after you met Brooke."

That muscle ticked in his jaw again, but now she'd started there was no way she would stop, not until she'd told him everything.

"Even then, I thought it might be an envy thing—my friend getting what I wanted so badly. And then I wondered if it was more about losing you as a friend, because the way I felt I couldn't talk to you any more. "

"I didn't ever cut you off, Angie."

"I know you didn't, not deliberately, but *I* felt cut off." Smiling sadly, she shook her head. "You were so besotted and always flying off to the city to see her, and when I did see you together I felt like my heart was being ripped out. I was afraid what I might say to you or Brooke."

"From memory, you did have your say."

"Down here? Yeah, I guess I did have a bit to say that night." She huffed out a breath, remembering. "It was a long time coming, though, because I kept questioning my motivation. What right did I have to caution you about marrying another woman when I wanted you for myself? Not that it stopped me."

She expected his agreement, some wry comment on her always saying her piece, but instead he looked steadily into her eyes and asked, "Is that why you didn't come to our wedding?"

"I couldn't," she said, and her voice shook with emotion. "I couldn't watch you together. I couldn't smile and play happy bridesmaid and catch the bouquet and pretend. The way I felt, Lord knows what I might have yelled out when the minister asked if anyone could show just cause."

Neither of them smiled. The atmosphere felt too intense, too grave, at complete odds with the perfect spring evening with its promise of a magical outback sunset.

"That's why you went away?" he asked.

She nodded. "And that's why I stayed away and why I didn't come home for Brooke's funeral. I felt too much of a hypocrite. I know that doesn't say much for me as a person or as a friend, but that's the truth."

He didn't say a word for a long, long while and despite the warmth of the sun, Angie rubbed her hands up and down her arms to ward off the sudden chill of his silence. She didn't have a clue what he was thinking. He picked up several pebbles from the ground at his feet and ran them through his fingers, and despite the intensity of the moment she couldn't stop watching the play of his hand, the slow stroke of his thumb.

"I can't give you what you're asking for, Angie." His voice, low and taut, shivered over her skin.

"Because of Brooke?"

"Yes." He studied the pebbles another second, then tossed them into the water. Angie watched the disturbance of their entry ripple across the water in ever-increasing rings until they disappeared altogether. And when he looked up again, Tomas's eyes were as mirror flat as that silver-blue surface. "You were right, Angie, what you said down here that night."

It took a moment for his meaning to gel, it was so unexpected. Angie swallowed hard—she had to in order to speak. "About Brooke fitting in?"

"She tried," he said after a beat of pause. "But she hated the time I spent away. Hated being alone, the isolation. The lack."

He didn't need to elucidate on that. Brooke had been a city girl through and through, slightly spoiled, not used to a lack of anything.

"You couldn't find some compromise?" she asked carefully. "A job she could do from—"

"She got a job," he said curtly. "In Broome. She'd applied, interviewed, without telling me. A done deal."

A surprise, Angie guessed, and why he didn't much like them.

"She told me the day she died." He looked up, and although his voice was flat, even, controlled, the look in his eyes was raw. "I can't go through that again, Angie. I don't have anything left to give."

"I'm not asking for anything."

"You are, Angie. I see it in your eyes and I hear it in your voice."

"No." Adamant, needing him to understand, to see into her heart, she leaned forward and made him look at her. "I only want you."

He stared back at her a moment. "Tell me you don't want to be my wife."

"I can't," she breathed, and in that moment she knew that her honesty would cost. Knew it would be her undoing.

"I can't marry you, Angie."

"I'm not asking for that commitment. I just want to stay, to live here with you." Her voice shook with the depth of her emotion. "I know about the isolation, I know how hard you work, and none of that fazes me. Give me a chance, Tomas, a chance to prove that this is the only place I want to be. Give me a chance to love you, that's all I want."

"I can't love you, Angie, and you deserve better than that."

Tomas made an appointment for her to see a doctor recommended by Alex—or Alex's secretary—the following week. Not a good time for him to be away, but he rearranged his schedule so he could go with her. She argued about whether that was necessary, but he stood his ground.

"It's my baby, too. I'm going to be there."

"Are you going to be there when he first starts to move? When she kicks? When he's born? Her first day—"

She'd made her point and he walked away. He wouldn't fight with her—what could be gained? The next day he flew to Brisbane to meet with some Japanese buyers, and when he returned three days later she was gone. He picked up the note she'd left in the middle of his bed, and scanned the words again.

I know you don't like surprises, so I am leaving this note. I want to see the doctor alone—if that's the way it will be in the future, then that's the way it should be now. I'll let you know when I have any news, either before or after the appointment. Love always, Angie.

He tried not to notice the quietness of a house without her vibrant presence, the loneliness of his dinner table, the skip of his pulse when he walked in the door half expecting to see her before he remembered…

She was gone, and wasn't that what he'd wanted all along?

Fourteen

The e-mail arrived the day before the doctor's appointment he'd made on her behalf, catching Tomas completely unprepared. He stared at the screen for five, ten, fifteen seconds while a herd of wild emotions stampeded through his system. When the thunder of his heartbeat receded to a bearable level he clicked on her name and opened the message.

It was short and to the point: she wasn't pregnant. She was very sorry she hadn't been able to help him, in any way. She wished him all the best.

No explanation of how she knew; no hint of how she'd taken the news; no sign that she felt anything like the hollow clenching disappointment in his gut.

Did she really think that a cold, unemotional e-mail was all he wanted from her? Hell, she hadn't even tempered the tone with a personal salutation. He stared at the signature line. *Angelina Mori, Corporate Conference Center, Carlisle Grande Hotel.*

She hadn't wasted any time asking Rafe for a new job. So much for her passionate I-love-the-outback vows. Evidently she'd slotted right back into the city. Clearly she didn't have time to call and tell him the news person to person. Obviously she had no idea how mad that would make him…or how worried because of all she hadn't said.

He didn't bother closing the e-mail or turning off the computer. He had a trip to plan.

By the time he arrived at the Carlisle Grande late that afternoon, Tomas had built up a full head of resentment, all of it justified. He was also tired, cranky, and edgy as a bullock in a branding race. It didn't help that Angie wasn't in her office, that he'd been led on a merry goose-chase through three levels of hotel facilities in an attempt to track her down. It didn't cross his mind to stay put and send a message. Sitting down was not an option.

He was a man on a mission, and when he stepped off the elevator—the fifth time—and caught sight of her at the far end of the ballroom he was in no mood for niceties.

The staff member who stepped into his path obviously was. "May I be of assistance, sir?"

"I'm here to see Angie," he said shortly.

"Do you mean Ms. Mori?"

Tomas ground his teeth. "Forget it, I'll go tell her myself."

"Is she expecting you?"

"I doubt it."

She was wearing the Ms. Hotel Management outfit, he noticed as he strode toward her, and looking all city-sleek and so damn beautiful that he had to work overtime to maintain his rage. Luckily it was a huge room. Luckily she was engrossed in conversation with a small cluster of pink-suited women and didn't notice his approach.

Then he heard the soft chuckle of her laughter and the impact of that sound caught thick in his chest. She was laughing? He'd dropped everything and rushed here because he was afraid for her emotional state after that terse un-Angie-like e-mail and *she was laughing?*

His temper seethed on the brink of control as he came to a halt several yards away, his gaze fixed on her smiling profile. He saw her stiffen slightly a second before she turned his way. Whatever she'd been saying froze on her lips and so did her smile. He was vaguely aware of the other women turning too, of all the chatter gradually fading into an intense, electric silence.

Only vaguely, though, because so much of his attention was focused on her face, on her full lips as they silently mouthed his name, on the surge of emotion that rocketed through his body. On stopping himself from walking over there, picking her up as he'd done that day in his bedroom, and carrying her off someplace private where he could rail and yell and then kiss her senseless.

Visibly she gathered herself and turned to murmur something to her group. Then she walked briskly off to the side and waited for him to catch up. "I'm busy," she said without preliminary. "If you could come back—"

"No, I couldn't."

She met his eyes for the first time, and he realized that she was working on her own head of steam. "I can't talk to you now. I'm working."

"I would be, too, if I wasn't here."

"Which brings us to why you are here," she said. "Didn't you get my e-mail?"

"Perhaps you could have called to check."

Her eyes narrowed. "You expected me to call? To what—discuss how many more ways you can tell me to get lost?"

"So I could ask how you are, how you're coping with the news. Whether there are any problems, healthwise."

"As you can see I'm fine," she said shortly and she started to turn away.

With a hand on her arm, he turned her back. "Are you, Angie? Are you fine?"

She drew a breath, released it on a sigh. "Yes, and I really do have work to do. I can't do this now, Tomas. Really, I can't."

He cast an irritated glance beyond her shoulder and caught a curious bunch of faces watching them intently. "How long will you be?"

"Twenty minutes but, frankly, I don't know what else there is to say…unless something has changed since last time we talked."

And there it was, the perfect opening. His chance to say…what? Had anything changed? Other than he'd recognized the fact that he missed her?

She made an impatient sound. "Does this visit have anything to do with Alex's wedding falling through? Or Rafe's new bride going AWOL?"

"No. I needed to know you're all right. With the pregnancy thing."

"We've established that I am," she said curtly, "because there is no pregnancy."

The cold impact of those words caught him unprepared, and he missed the cue by a mile. She turned out of his hold and started walking away, each tap of her heels on the timber floor a brisk note of finality. A sick, scary feeling settled in Tomas's gut. He'd been here before and got it all wrong, was he going to do the same again? Was he going to let the woman he loved walk away because he was too stubborn and too scared and too tongue-tied to say what needed to be said?

"It's not only about the pregnancy," he called out after her, and he sensed a dozen eyes fix onto his face. Not one of them was dark and luminous and fired with passion or seething with anger. The only eyes that mattered remained steadfastly turned away and she kept on walking.

"Unless you want me to shout the rest of what I have to say across the room, Angie, you better stop walking away."

A thousand emotions pounded through Angie's blood as she heard and barely dared to believe what she'd heard. She stopped, drew a deep breath. "This had better be good, Tomas Carlisle, and it better not cost me my job."

"You want to keep this job?" he asked.

Slowly she turned and met his eyes. Her heart kicked hard in her chest. "It's not my first choice."

"The commute would be tough."

"If I were living…?"

"With me." He took the first steps, as slow and steady and deliberate as the blue eyes that held hers, and her heart started singing with joy. "We miss you, Angie."

"We?"

"Manny and Rae miss you giving them nights off. Stink says you're the only one who listens to his stories. Charlie misses the long walks."

"And you?"

He stopped in front of her. "More than anyone."

"What are you saying, Tomas Carlisle?"

"I want you to come home, Angie." He touched her face with one hand. "I want to take that chance you offered me."

"You said I deserve better."

"I said a lot of things that day. Most of them I thought I meant, some of them I even believed." He swallowed, shifted his feet, frowned. "I'm not good with expressing how I feel, especially with an audience—" he cast a glowering glance at the small gallery of spectators and she heard a murmur of voices and a shuffling of high heels "—but I want to be that better man you deserve."

For a moment she was too overwhelmed by his words to speak, so she turned her face into his hand and kissed the palm. *You are that man,* she thought, *you are.* And just when she thought she might find her voice, to tell him so, he traced her lower lip with his thumb and said, "I love you, Angie."

Not so bad, she decided when she could think again, for a man short on words to express himself. And she told him so before he kissed her, and after he kissed her she told him that she loved him, that she always had, that she always would.

"Are you sorry about the baby?" Tomas asked.

"We still have time to try again, to make sure we keep Kameruka." He didn't miss the *we.* He liked the way that sounded. Their home, their future, as partners. "Third time is supposed to be lucky."

"No," he said, smiling into her eyes. "I'm lucky."

Twenty-five minutes later, after she'd dispersed her Pink Ladies and finished her working day, they walked hand in hand to the best suite in the hotel and as soon as he closed the door she walked into his arms and he got very, very lucky.

* * * * *

COMING NEXT MONTH

#1669 MISTAKEN FOR A MISTRESS—Kristi Gold
Dynasties: The Ashtons
To solve his grandfather's murder, Ford Ashton concealed his true identity to seduce his grandfather's suspected mistress. But he soon discovered that Kerry Rourke was not all *she* appeared to be. Her offer to help him find the truth turned his mistrust to attraction. Yet even if they solved the case, could love survive with so much deception between them?

#1670 HOT TO THE TOUCH—Jennifer Greene
Fox Lockwood was suffering from a traumatic war experience no doctor could cure. Enter Phoebe Schneider—a masseuse specializing in soothing distraught infants. But Fox was fully grown, and though Phoebe desired to relieve his tension, dare she risk allowing their professional relationship to take a more personal turn?

#1671 LESS-THAN-INNOCENT INVITATION—Shirley Rogers
Texas Cattleman's Club: The Secret Diary
When Melissa Mason heard rancher Logan Voss proposed to her simply to secure his family inheritance, she ended their engagement and broke his heart. Ten years later, now an accomplished news reporter, Melissa had accepted an assignment that brought her back to Logan, forcing her to confront the real reason she left all they had behind.

#1672 ROCK ME ALL NIGHT—Katherine Garbera
King of Hearts
Dumped by her fiancé on New Year's Eve, late-night DJ Lauren Belchoir had plenty to vent to her listeners about romance. But when hip record producer Jack Montrose appeared, passion surged between them like high-voltage ariwaves. Would putting their hearts on the air determine if their fairy-tale romance was real, or just after-hours gossip?

#1673 SEDUCTION BY THE BOOK—Linda Conrad
The Gypsy Inheritance
Widower Nicholas Scoville had isolated himself on his Caribbean island—until beautiful Annie Riley arrived and refused to be ignored. One long night, one vivid storm and some mindless passion later…could what they found in each other's arms overcome Nick's painful past?

#1674 HER ROYAL BED—Laura Wright
She had been a princess only a month before yearning for her old life. So when Jane Hefner Al-Nayhal traveled to Texas to see her brother and a detour landed her in the arms of cowboy Bobby Callahan, she began thinking of taking a permanent vacation. But Bobby had planned to destroy her family. Was Jane's love strong enough to prevent disaster?

SDCNM0705